Blurring the Lines

Brad Center

authorHOUSE®

AuthorHouse™
1663 Liberty Drive
Bloomington, IN 47403
www.authorhouse.com
Phone: 1 (800) 839-8640

Published by AuthorHouse 12/06/2018

ISBN: 978-1-5462-6889-5 (sc)
ISBN: 978-1-5462-6888-8 (hc)
ISBN: 978-1-5462-6887-1 (e)

Library of Congress Control Number: 2018913694

Print information available on the last page.

This book is printed on acid-free paper.

Contents

Author's Note

Is our reality constant, consistent, and never changing? Even as the question is asked, we must then consider the logical follow up question. Whose reality? For surely, our reality is built upon our perceptions and senses that help us interpret how we see and perceive the world around us. Using that as a starting point, the questions flow like some metaphysical game of "What's My Line?" Is my reality the same as a man who is blind and has never seen a sunset? Is the reality of a Buddhist monk in Tibet the same as a banker in Amsterdam? Does the reality of Bill Gates in 2018 remotely resemble that of a farmer in Midwest America circa 1840?

That's the heart of it—our reality may not be as hard and intractable as we may first believe, and our dreams could, in fact, mark the boundaries of our conscious world. Given that as a jumping off point, the stories that follow attempt to turn our reality sideways. They seek to challenge our acceptance of our everyday world. These stories walk up to the edge of what we perceive and sometimes they even jump off the cliff. They lead to the land of "What If." The land of "What If" is not always the most comfortable place, but it's a place of possibilities—at least for some.

With that, I invite you inside the dark recesses of my psyche, but please take note:

The ancient doorbell rings, fastened upon its crusted frame
Atonal chords float upon vapors in the feeble light
Desiccated husks then stir and rise
Greeting those seeking
Entrance

Of course, on the brighter side there are always the words of the great Mark Twain who said, "Reality can be beaten with enough imagination."

Brad Center, November 2018

Acknowledgements

I want to thank my wife Valerie for her continued support and encouragement as I worked to put pen to paper (as the outdated saying goes) and continued this journey. Wrestling with these ideas and characters has had its fits and starts—getting from here to there does not always follow a straightforward path, but with her help and guidance, this part of the journey is now complete. I also want to thank my friends (Richard Kosoff, Rick Rosenburg, Lisa Talcott, and Greg Cioffi) for their feedback as I pitched ideas and concepts their way. Their input was and is greatly appreciated. A huge thank you to Linda Kosoff for the creation of the book cover. She took some simple ideas of mine and created something that is both haunting and beautiful.

I also have to thank my editor Dara Light for her valuable assistance because (let's be honest here) I am editorially challenged. I also need to thank my wife Valerie for her editorial comments and suggestions as well. To both I say, "I really am trying to improve my ability to put a comma in the right place—truly I am." Their edits and suggestions made this book a reality.

Lastly, I want to salute the great writers of speculative, science and horror fiction who have influenced me and whose works I have savored as they poured forth from their collective imaginations. I especially want to pay tribute to those great writers who are no longer with us, like Isaac Asimov, Arthur C. Clarke, Harlan Ellison, Philip K Dick, Lester Del Ray, Ursula K. Le Guin, and others, we (the world's readers) are eternally in your debt. To those who continue to churn out great fiction in these fields, please, never stop! You help us see the world

Brad Center

through a unique and powerful lens and we need you in these strange and uncertain times.

"It's all in the telling. . ."
—Anonymous

Introduction to
Revelation No. 2 – In the Ending. . .

L et's begin with a couple of simple questions. First, if you had an
eternity to kill, how would you pass the time? Think on that for a
minute. . . Now, a second question: if the universe gave you a second
chance, what would you do with it? Of course, the universe can be a
fickle gift giver, so beware.

"Reality leaves a lot to the imagination."
—John Lennon

Revelation No. 2 – In the Ending. . .

The alarm goes off. A reminder of sorts—signaling the time to decide. All things come to an end, really, they do. I've given things plenty of time to play out down there. Should I pull the plug on the entire thing? No, I think I will hit the snooze button and think on it for a few.

<u>Book I: Killing Time Before the Apocalypse</u>

"For Pete's sake, would you deal the damn cards!" exclaimed Death.

"OK, OK, hold your horses, I'm dealing," answered Pestilence.

"Is that supposed to be funny?" replied Death.

Pestilence looked at Death for a second, a small smile creeping across his face, and then dealt the cards. Five card draw was Pestilence's favorite game and so he dealt five cards each to Death, War, Famine and himself.

The Four Horsemen were seated around the card table playing a seemingly never-ending game of poker. Pestilence was drinking a glass of milk. He didn't drink alcohol. War had a glass of Merlot by his side. Famine was drinking coffee and Death had a glass of Chardonnay in his hand. They liked to stay in character at all times, and the symbolism represented by the color of each beverage suited them.

They sat in what appeared to be an old west saloon from America circa the 1840s. It was a complete mental fabrication created by Death from his memories of that era. Before that, they had been in a European styled parlor—one of Famine's creations. Before that it had been a Roman market and before that, well who could remember for sure? They had been playing cards, or a similar game, for eons. They were biding their time, waiting to be called.

It was Famine's turn to deal. He paused and waited for everyone's attention. Famine tended to be overly dramatic. Perhaps it was because he was dressed in all black. It was a striking look, everyone said so. Finally, he said, "I think the time draws near."

"Stop being so melodramatic!" responded War. "I think the time draws near," he continued, mocking Famine's more formal speech pattern.

Famine replied, "I am not being dramatic. I am simply stating my belief. You may take a contrary point of view if you so desire, but I have stated my opinion for the record."

Pestilence glared at both of them. "Can we focus on the game please? I've been cleaning up the entire century, and you guys just can't stand it."

"The century is less than 20 years old my friend. I wouldn't get too comfortable just yet," replied Death. "I have a feeling I'm about to get lucky."

Famine dealt the cards for a new game of seven card stud. As Famine dealt, he repeated his statement and asked if anyone agreed with him.

Death considered the question, and eventually said, "I suppose it could be the end. But we've been through this before. Remember the Spanish Flu that infected nearly a third of the world's population and killed about 50 million people? Or what about the Cuban Missile Crisis? That could have done it as well, if someone had gotten an itchy trigger finger!"

"By the way, hats off to you guys," Death continued, pointing at War and Pestilence for their most recent efforts. "If I were a betting man, and it seems that I am, given our current poker game, then I would have bet we were on the verge of getting called to our posts on either of those occasions. But here we remain."

As the rest of the Four Horseman considered Death's words, Death quietly won the hand. "I told you not to get your hopes up Pesty, I knew I was about to get hot."

"Yeah, yeah," said Pestilence. "And you know how I hate it when you call me Pesty!" Death just smiled.

Looking directly at Death, Pestilence said, "I suppose Famine could be right though, I mean the Americans just elected "Mr. Reality TV" as their President. If you were looking for a sign, that seems like a good one to me, but hey, I'm just one of the Four Horseman, what do I know?"

"Kind of fits the whole false prophet thing if you ask me," added War. Setting down his glass of wine, he continued, "But no real sense in debating it boys, when we get called, we get called. For now, let's play some cards."

There was general agreement around the room to that. Death continued his winning streak, but War won a few hands as well. Famine and Pestilence were definitely on a run of bad luck. At some point, Pestilence turned to Death, "By the way, there's something I've always wanted to ask you."

"What's that?"

"Well, here we are, all pretty fearsome and all, so what I want to know is why you get to be Death."

Famine jumped in before Death could answer. "I agree" he said. "After all, I am decked out in all black. It would seem only natural that I should represent death. As you may know, the Greeks believed that your spirit went to the Underworld where all is darkness and black. And let's not forget the Romans, who started the custom of wearing all black at funerals. I could go on, but I believe the point is made."

Death shot them both a look appropriate to his name and character. "I will have you know, that in many non-western cultures, including many Asian and African cultures, white, or in my case, a pale coloring is the traditional color associated with death. However, in truth, none of what the humans say or do matters all that much. Our fates were decided by another, and I think you know who I mean. Do any of you feel like making a formal complaint?"

"I was just asking," said Pestilence. "No need to get all huffy."

They played on. Hours, weeks, and months may have passed as the cards were dealt and the chips changed hands. Time worked in a different sort of way for the Four Horseman. They took little notice.

It was War's turned to deal. War tended to call some very silly card games, like seven card stud, with One-Eyed Jacks and the Suicide King wild. He could be a tad juvenile when it pleased him. Just look at the Hundred Years' War! If you are going to name something the Hundred Years' War, you would think it would last a hundred years, but War helped drag it on an additional 16 years just for kicks.

War was, at heart, a restless soul. Thoughts churned inside him like a cement mixer, tossing and turning inside his brain, waiting to pour out when needed. So, without much thought or concern where the conversation might lead, he turned to the other Horsemen and asked, "Why do humans continue to do such stupid shit?"

"You're going to need to be more specific," replied Pestilence. "That's a pretty general condemnation, and yes, they do a lot of stupid shit."

War nodded and then explained. "Granted there are a lot of stupid things they do, but it's their need," he paused for a moment to consider that thought, "no, change that, it's their compulsion to be right about everything that I think drives so much of their heartache—at least that is how it seems to me. Remember, they spend a lot of time killing each other in war, so I get to spend a lot of time down there. Anyway, there is not a human down on that silly planet who doesn't feel the absolute desire to be right about every stupid-ass thing they say or do. When you think about it, it seems to be the cause of just about every other problem they suffer from."

"I see what you are saying," said Famine. "They wander around down there seeking some type of purpose to their little lives and to make their short existence palatable, they need to feel important, different, unique. So, they fight to the death to defend anything they say or do. Every utterance, every action is all they have."

"Yes, I think that is a fairly good summary," said War.

"So, what do you suggest," asked Pestilence, "that we provide some type of global psycho-therapy session for all humanity?"

"Not my circus and they are certainly not my monkeys," War replied, repeating the old adage with a smile.

"So, it's not your job?" asked Pestilence.

War nodded his head, "Exactly."

"And that, my friends, is the real answer," replied Death.

"Come again?" queried War.

"Well, consider the four of us. We know our role. We know our purpose. There is no ambiguity with us. We don't need to justify all we say and do because we know who and what we are. If our human friends had more defined roles or understood their collective role a little better, then maybe they would be better off. They would stop trying to validate their own existence every moment. If they understood this simple fact, they would stop trying to be right every second and hurt each other a lot less."

"You think it's that simple?" asked War.

"Yes, I do," said Death.

The conversation ended just that simply. During this conversation, the card game never halted. They played on without commenting on the game easily enough. A few more games passed, when War once again jump-started the conversation.

"Gentlemen, I've been wondering. We all have a pretty good idea what will happen to the humans down there when we hop on our horses and start riding, but I wonder what exactly will happen to us when our work is done. I mean the Book seems to be a little skimpy on that. It might be the end for us, you know."

"That's an interesting and thoughtful question," said Pestilence. "I'm surprised you came up with it."

"Fuck off," said War.

"Now let's keep things clean and professional," said Famine. "I hate it when you use guttural language," he said, staring at War.

"Never mind the language. He could've used Aramaic or Etruscan for all I care. The fact is, his point is well taken," declared Death.

"We really don't know what happens to us after we ride our way into apocalyptic history," said War.

"So, what do you think happens?" asked Famine as he looked at each of the Horsemen.

After a while Death said, "I guess there are a myriad of possibilities. Remember, as we just discussed, we were created to serve a purpose but consider this: there are many worlds in this universe and while we currently associate ourselves with the humans on planet Earth, there is no reason to conclude that we would not also be needed on other planets at some point. We aren't human per se, we represent specific concepts. I think Death, War, Pestilence, and Famine are universal ideas. These ideas, and therefore we ourselves are not applicable only to Earth."

He paused as the Horsemen nodded in agreement. This was one of the longer speeches Death had ever made and the others took note. Then Death continued, clearly on a roll. "Let's also consider the possibility of multiple universes. I think we all remember when Schrödinger first postulated the concept back in the 1950s. Quite a good lecture as I recall. I think we were all there except War who was off overseeing events in Korea at the time."

"Hey, I had a job to do!" interjected War.

"No issues, my good friend, we all understood," responded Death. He then continued, "Anyway, I think the science is pretty strong in favor of a multiverse as I see it. All in all, I think our prospects are quite promising."

After a while, the card game began again, and things settled down. Everything was quiet for a time. Eventually, mindless chatter once again entered their interactions and everything was back to normal for the Horsemen.

Then, suddenly Death's phone rang. The phone was just as much a mental fabrication as the saloon was, but Death liked to keep up with the times and so he had contrived the device should "The Call" come during this time period. As Death took the phone from his pocket, the old west saloon faded out of existence. The other Horsemen stood at attention. They knew what this meant, and they waited for Death to respond to the call.

Slowly he put the phone to his ear. The others could hear Death as he spoke to their creator. "Yes," he said, "We are all here. Is it time?" He nodded to the voice. "Really, so that's how it ends! Wow, I never would have guessed. Really, never. I can't wait to tell Pestilence; I think he will be amused. We will saddle right up. Thank you."

Death paused, still holding the phone to his ear, "Ah, may I ask a question of you?" He waited for a response, "Oh, you were listening to our conversation? I should have guessed. What's that? We do have more work to do after this is over? Oh, that is very good to hear, thank you. We are pleased to be of service."

Death turned off the phone, "Well boys, you heard it. Time to ride." The other Horsemen stood motionless. They were ready, but still they did not move. Death turned to them, "Well?"

Eventually it was Pestilence who spoke, "What did you mean when you said that you were surprised how it ends, and that I would be amused?"

Death replied, "Oh that. Well, it seems that our creator does work in mysterious ways after all, and as I am sure you know, has a flair for the dramatic. You'll never guess what's going on down on earth right now while we have been playing cards."

War responded, "No we can't guess. Tell us!"

"It's a virus, and it has taken over the planet. It's prion-based and seems to mimic (in many ways) those silly zombie films and books that are so prevalent these days. Well, maybe not so silly in retrospect. I didn't get a ton of specifics on the phone but if there really are zombies down there, I have got to see that for myself. The humans are freaking out and so we better get a move on."

"I told you,' he said looking at Pestilence, "that you would love it."

Pestilence smiled, knowing it was his gift that started the end. Certainly, war and famine would accompany a zombie styled plague, and of course death always followed, but it was nice to know his special gift had been what the creator had used to begin the apocalypse. It was good to know your work was appreciated.

Death turned to his fellow Horsemen, "Let's do what we must, and as I think you heard, job security is not going to be an issue."

Book II: An Organizational Manifesto for the Recently Undead

I'm a fucking zombie. It sucks. I don't care what anyone tells you—walking around all day and eating human flesh is a shitty way to spend your after-life, or after-death in my case. There is never time to rest, to talk (not that we can talk now), or even take a bath. God, I want a bath. I smell like death warmed over—literally.

I guess I should start at the beginning and bring you up to speed. I was a manager at FedEx and pretty damned good at my job. Of course, that was before all hell broke loose. I oversaw our Beltsville Maryland hub. It was my job to make sure packages were delivered safely and efficiently to our customers and to make sure our personnel were safe and effective in their jobs.

Now I am a zombie, and I meander aimlessly looking for my next meal of human flesh. Not exactly a promotion! What's the point? Instinct drives me onward despite my internal loathing of my current circumstances.

I guess it was about three months ago that the epidemic struck. I was never really into science. Logistics was more my thing, so I really didn't understand too much of what I was reading in the papers. Of course, eventually the newspapers and TV disappeared without so much as a test pattern or final edition. Before they disappeared, I remembered reading something about a new virus strain and something to do with prions—whatever the fuck they are. Anyway, the infection spread like wildfire and soon people were turning into zombies all over the world. It would have been funny if it weren't so horrible, because it was just like Hollywood had imagined. Zombies were roaming around on pure instinct trying to eat non-infected people. It was right out of a B movie. At least that is how it looked as a human.

Now, of course, it looks quite different being one of the undead. Contrary to popular belief, we are not without the capability of higher thought. But, once you are infected, you are possessed by Zombie Instinct. Zombie Instinct seems to operate at some super heightened level. When it kicks in—when you smell the uninfected—you are simply compelled to move and then to eat. It's disgusting, I know, but there you have it. But, all of that is happening on the outside. On the inside, at least in my head, things are quite different. Inside, I feel pretty much the same as I did when I was human. Until I smell the living that is. Then, I admit things get a little foggy.

Life as a zombie is repetitious and exhausting. I have been undead for a while now, and I have seen things that would make you laugh, vomit, or shock the shit of you—sometimes all at the same time. One of these moments happened not long after I turned. I was walking outside Washington, D.C., and I bumped into the Vice President of the United States. He was one of us —a zombie VIP. I guess technically he might still be considered the Vice President, though I'm pretty sure the Constitution never included any provisions for the undead in succession planning. Anyway, the Veep was a zombie now. I have no idea how he succumbed to his fate, perhaps the Secret Service had their hands full and figured the Vice President was just a tad expendable. I can't be sure.

Anyway, we were jostling down Massachusetts Avenue in D.C. when we ran into what looked like a full army battalion. There were about 300 soldiers, and once they saw us, they opened fire. I am not sure how many of us were there on the street, but we started dropping like flies. However, we outnumbered them and instinct drove us on into the line of fire. While hundreds of us fell, we eventually reached the army's front line. As soon as that happened, it was all over for them. We fell on them. Those that were not completely devoured (I will spare you the gross parts), were immediately turned into more zombies. If only the army had such recruiting prowess!

The Vice President was by my side through most of it. In fact, we reached the front line together. You should have seen the look on the soldiers' faces as the VP advanced on them—an odd mix of fear and confusion. Training told them to shoot and protect in the same instant.

Then, the VP fell on them and started chewing. That pretty much melted away any "protect" training, and they blew the Vice President's head right off. I guess I owe my undead life to the Vice President because he diverted their attention from me and my own little zombie plight.

But my plight, however trivial in the grand scheme of things, seems very real to me. I worked for FedEx for crying out loud! We were a well-oiled machine. We had plans and a purpose. I loved it. I am very much a "right-brain" kind of guy, even as a zombie. Individually, now I wander aimlessly and as the zombie species (for surely, we must be considered a separate and distinct species now), we are purposeless.

One of my biggest frustrations is our inability to communicate with each other. It seems that during the transition we have effectively lost the ability to speak. You humans seem to think we have lost all higher cognitive powers because we do not speak, but that just isn't true or at least it's not true for me. All I can do is grunt and groan a little. It's all terribly frustrating.

Time moves on and a few more months have passed. I am learning to come to grips with my zombie-hood. I still hate eating human flesh. I mean, it's horrific but a guy's gotta eat, doesn't he? I am still frustrated, and this may sound strange, but my frustration stems from my growing acceptance of my current situation. Let me explain.

I am a zombie. It still isn't great, but it is who I am now. But I still get frustrated by our lack of communication and organization. There must be a better way! My instinct and training when I was alive centered on order and structure. Am I asking too much to bring some modicum of purpose to this existence?

The key must be some type of communication. If I could communicate with my fellow zombies then, from there, I could develop relationships, perhaps even friendships. Then we could get organized, but first things first, I need to find a way to communicate.

Over the past few weeks I've been playing around with a type of simple sign language. I remembered that a few years ago a friend of mine at FedEx adopted a daughter who had some significant disabilities and could not speak. To communicate with her, they used a simplified form of American Sign Language. It employed easy hand movements and simple concepts, but no alphabet. I was close with my friend and visited his house often enough that I picked up some of this sign language—enough to try with my fellow zombies.

For the past week or so there has been one particular zombie constantly by my side. I am not sure why he has stayed near me, but he seems like a fine fellow—I mean in a zombie-ish kind of way. I have named him Tate, and I've decided to teach Tate the new zombie sign language.

Why did I decide to name him Tate? Well, when I was a kid, my parents got me a beagle. It was my first dog, and I loved that little fellow. He was loyal, had a great nose for food, and howled like only a good beagle can. We grew up together, Tate and I. However, Tate started to slow down as he got older and eventually Tate got cancer. My parents knew how much the dog meant to me, so they paid some serious coin and got Tate chemo treatments. But in the end, the cancer finally got him. He died just nine months after he was diagnosed with the dreaded disease. He was only eight years old when he left me. I cried for what seemed like a very long time.

Zombie Tate simply reminded me a lot of my dog. He was loyal, and he never seemed to leave my side. He too had a nose for food. In his case, he could smell the uninfected miles away. Lastly, like Tate the dog, Zombie Tate had a limited vocal repertoire—just grunts and groans not too dissimilar to a beagle's bark. So, Tate it was.

Tate was a slow learner. It took three weeks before he grasped the basics of the new Zombie Sign Language. But eventually we were communicating to a degree. He learned the signs for stop, wait, come, happy, hungry, angry, human, run, and others. I also made up a sign for "zombie" so we could differentiate ourselves from the humans through signing.

However slow, the fact that Tate learned sign language seemed to confirm that we zombies retain some mental capacity. It appeared that I kept more mental capacity than Tate, and perhaps other zombies, but there seemed to be enough zombie-thought left for us to communicate. If we could communicate, we could organize. If we organized, the humans did not stand a chance.

Zombie-life is slowly getting better. I admit it will never equal my old life. I will never again see a good movie, enjoy a deep meaningful conversation, or go out to a nice dinner. Those things are dead and gone. I miss all of that and more, but the memories are fading, and I have a new life now. I am part of a new species. One that is destined to succeed man just as Homo Sapiens succeeded Neanderthals.

The Zombie Sign Language I developed has spread quickly over our population. We now communicate fairly well in small groups. In addition to Tate, I found other zombie disciples. I've taught them not only the Zombie Sign Language but also some basic guiding principles. My disciples have spread these ideas to other tribes of zombies and have taken leadership roles with these other tribes. I taught them what I like to call our Organizational Manifesto. The Manifesto has three basic rules: Control, Capture, Conquer.

Zombie Rule Number One – Control: While we cannot resist the impulse to hunt the uninfected, we do not have to completely devour every human we meet on the streets. If we eat a human down to the bone, they end up making a lousy zombie and eventually just fall apart. Yes, we must eat, but we also must show some self-control. Eat but don't gorge. Leave enough so that the human turns and joins us as another functional zombie.

Zombie Rule Number Two – Capture: We need to capture humans for breeding purposes. If we turn every human we meet into a zombie right away, then soon enough, we will run out of food. I guess that must sound horrible and gross, but you must remember we are a different species and we have a right to survive. Was it gross when a lion killed an antelope? Was it horrible when humans bred cattle? I guess if you were a vegan you thought it was disgusting, but I wasn't and so this makes perfect sense to me.

Zombie Rule Number Three – Conquer: We need to divide and conquer. We cannot swarm in mass numbers where the humans can bomb or otherwise use weapons of mass destruction upon us. We must spread out in manageable groups. We can avoid major losses in this manner and can communicate more effectively with our simplified sign language.

Slowly, inexorably, using these principles we are winning. It helps that the humans naturally fear us. They seem to lose all rational thought as we approach. I can't say I blame them. We are a fearsome force.

We attack in small groups, we feed on some and gather other humans for our breeding camps. The humans still have no idea that we are organized. Unlike some silly Hollywood film, there is no brave scientist, who, fighting against all odds, has figured out a cure or a way to defeat us. Sorry humans, this zombie story ends differently.

So, in the end, I am a zombie and that's just fine with me. We are in control of this world now, and I guess I am kind of the head zombie. Slowly, I have re-learned the ability to write. It's slow and tedious with my less than stellar zombie dexterity, but I can do it. I leave this journal for any humans that might be left outside our breeding camps. I leave this journal with no apologies. I never asked for this life, I don't think any of us did. We are simply what came next evolutionarily speaking. If you're smart, you will stay out of our way!

Once you master the art of communication and get your team organized there is nothing you cannot accomplish. I learned that at FedEx. Once again, I am focused on efficiency and effectiveness. I have a plan and a purpose, and I love it!

A decision made, but not the end. No, not really. Not the end for the Horsemen and not the end for everything down on earth. A change, surely, but not the end. Admittedly humans are in a bad way, but those zombies are making great strides. Glad to have helped with that. Sometimes all it takes is one person or zombie, to make the difference.

No, not the end at all, rather a new chapter or perhaps a whole new book.

Introduction to
Shift Change

Perhaps we control our own destiny. Perhaps, a kind and gentle deity looks over us from on high, and provides just the right amount of guidance, love and support. Then again, probably not. Perhaps, just perhaps, our destinies and our beliefs are intertwined in some strange manner or to put it another way...

"Reality is not always probable, or likely."
— Jorge Luis Borges

Shift Change

The elevator door opened, and Felix, Marie, and Seymour walked into the Control Room. They looked around to find the room bustling with activity as the last shift completed their final duties. At the controls were Milton, Henry, and Randolph. They finished their final checks and recorded the last readouts from the Perception and Conviction display screens high atop the Control Room floor.

Hearing the new team enter the Control Room, Henry looked back over his shoulder. He looked up from the hand-held device he was holding. "Welcome! We'll be done shortly. Have a seat over there," he said, motioning to the chairs in the rear of the room. "Make yourselves comfortable. There are doughnuts in the corner if you want something to eat. Milton and I have a bit of a sweet tooth, so we indulge. Randolph, well, not so much." He said the last bit, looking over his shoulder with a wry smile at Randolph. Randolph, busy at his control station, looked up briefly and nodded.

Felix, Marie and Seymour sat down as instructed and watched closely. None of them even looked at the doughnuts. They were rather serious types and considered the doughnuts a frivolous non-nutritional waste. They were representatives of Science in its purest form and did not indulge in frivolous behavior. It was just not who they were as individuals or as a group.

The Control Room was not anywhere or anywhen in particular. It existed, but not in any way that was comprehensible to humans. Down on earth, time moved forward in a predictable pattern, but in the Control Room, time had little meaning. At this moment, as humans measured time, it was the middle of the 20th century; and at this moment in human history, science was the modern elixir of prosperity, happiness, and security. It was the age of nuclear power, relativity theory, jet engines, antibiotics, quantum mechanics, radio, and television. The personal computer, the internet, smart phones, artificial intelligence, robotics and genetic engineering were still on the horizon, but their appearance on the scientific stage would only cement the devout, energetic, and all-encompassing belief in the wonders of science.

Such a belief was catalogued and noted by *The Management.* They saw the shift, for it was their duty to do so, and promptly dispatched a new crew to the Control Room—in this case the team of Felix, Marie and Seymour. This was not the first such change to come to the Control Room. No, there had been many, and perhaps more to come. Felix, Marie and Seymour were the physical embodiment of the modern scientific age. They were professional, smart, detail-oriented, no-nonsense individuals who believed in the scientific method as others had once believed in ancient religious texts. They would take the controls from Milton, Henry, and Randolph who had been on duty for the last two hundred years or so—ever since the beginning of the Industrial Age monitoring all earthly activity. It was their job not only to monitor all activity, but to actively foster and encourage a belief in industry and commerce as the preeminent belief system around the world. They accomplished this feat through continuous and subtle manipulations to earthly events that resulted in the growth of industry and commerce and the recognition of these benefits by humans across the globe

Not long ago, as humans measure time, they had arranged for a shopkeeper to prominently display a set of pocket watches in his storefront window. They arranged this knowing that a young man would pass such a display and likely purchase a pocket watch for his son. This boy would then dismantle and reassemble the timepiece repeatedly as he grew into adulthood. In doing so, he would gain an appreciation for engineering and precision. Eventually he would develop and install the first moving assembly line. That boy was Henry Ford.

It was not that they could see into the future, but they could, with the help of the algorithms built into the Control Room, see possibilities. Some of their manipulations came to nothing, but others moved mankind towards a conviction that industry and commerce were the foundations of the "good life." Milton, Henry, and Randolph used the Perception and Conviction displays in the Control Room to monitor and measure the strength of this belief at any given time.

But human beings are fickle beasts and no single belief system rules forever. Certainly, there are *True Believers*, whose belief never wavers, and who are the standard bearers for their faith. Religions, for example, have long lives, but they do not necessarily control the outcome of human events throughout every eon. There was a period in human history where religion was the dominant belief system, and a team was dispatched to the Control Room to monitor and foster religious beliefs. But that time had long since passed.

Management was diligent, and when the Perception and Conviction displays indicated that a belief system had waned sufficiently, a new team was dispatched in time to help foster the new belief system. *Management* knew that humans needed to believe in something. The absence in a belief system made humans anxious and uncomfortable. They were like small children separated from their parents at a county fair. Keep them separated for too long, and those feelings of discomfort would turn to fear and desperation, and then all sorts of bad things could happen. It was best to keep them placated through these belief systems. Of course, *The Management* had to be careful because if the belief in any particular system spiked too high, then humans lost the ability to act rationally. This occurred from time to time and with disastrous consequences. Therefore, the Perception and Conviction displays had to be monitored extremely carefully.

Henry and his team completed their final checks and stood up. "Time for us to move on," he said. "You will need to calibrate the displays to the specific belief system you will be monitoring, but I gather you know that."

Felix, Marie, and Seymour nodded in unison. *Management* had briefed them appropriately. "We are ready to begin our watch," Marie said matter-of-factly.

"OK then, we will get out of your hair. Oh, before I forget, you may want to keep an eye on the whole nuclear issue. The humans are very into it right now, but we don't want them blowing themselves up—at least I don't think we want that to happen. You never can tell what *Management* really wants. We just do what we are told. Right?" He smiled, looked up, and shrugged his shoulders in a combined movement that gave him a somewhat impish quality.

"We appreciate that," responded Seymour without much emotion.

It was like receiving a poorly written greeting card from a distant cousin, thought Henry. It was meant to convey some emotion but fell as flat as a pancake. As representatives of the scientific method, Seymour, Marie, and Felix were not unfeeling, but were unaccustomed to expressing feelings in such a public manner.

Seymour continued, "We were asked to convey our appreciation for your service. You've done a splendid job these last couple of centuries."

"Well, we've had a good run. Not as long as some, but a good run nevertheless," said Randolph. Milton, Henry, and Randolph then picked up their belongings, shook hands with the new team, got into the elevator and ascended. Their shift had ended.

"Well gentleman," said Marie, "shall we get down to business?" While there was no official leader amongst the three, Marie was the most natural in a command role, and Felix and Seymour had no complaints following her lead.

"Seymour, can you see what we have on a young boy named Craig Venter? The read-outs I am looking at suggest, interestingly enough, that getting him drafted into the army and sent to Vietnam will lead to an active interest in medicine. If we push ever so gently this could bear fruit in human genome mapping down the road."

"I'll get right on that, Marie."

"Felix, can you look into alternative energy sources we can promote? Henry was right, we don't want them blowing themselves up, at least not on our watch."

"Already on it."

The team settled down to their various tasks and watched as their actions began to influence human events, and time passed. The Perception and Conviction displays reflected their impact by slowly climbing. When Marie and her team took over from the Industry and Commerce Team, the charts were already on the rise, but now their subtle manipulations began to have a noticeable impact in the human belief in science. It was gratifying work for the team.

"Marie, do you have a minute to look over this read-out?" asked Seymour. Marie bent over Seymour's shoulder and looked at the display. "I see what the issue is. You just need to make sure Neil de Grasse Tyson goes to Cornell. There he should meet Carl Sagan and that should keep him on the path we want for him."

"OK, I see what you mean. That should do it. While I have your attention, I've been meaning to ask you about something Henry and his team mentioned before they left the Control Room."

"What's that?" asked Marie.

"When Henry was leaving he said that their run had not been as long as some others. Do you remember him saying that?"

"Yes, I recall. So, what?"

"Well, I don't mean to sound stupid, but what exactly did he mean by that?"

"Did you fall asleep during the orientation briefings, Seymour?" Marie asked, a little exasperated.

"No, well not exactly, but lectures always bore me. You know that. I guess my mind wandered a bit."

"You know that we are here for as long as science and the scientific method are the leading belief system down on earth, right?"

"Sure, but how far back does *Management's* influence go?"

"Ah, well, that goes back pretty far—pretty much back to the time of recorded history. In early times, we were considered gods, although they did not know us by name, but rather by what we represented. If my memory serves me correctly, and I think it does, the first to operate the Control Room were the Gods of the Elements—fire, water, earth, air. Again, they were just like us, and so calling any of us 'gods' is a bit of a stretch, but you get the point. After that *Religion* took hold as the dominant belief system. Religion held humanity's imagination for a long time, and that team had a long shift in the Control Room. After that, came the era of *Conquest*. A very bloody time indeed. Is any of this ringing a bell, Seymour?"

"Yes, but go on."

"Well, there is not much more to tell. As humans' lust for conquest diminished, they yearned to explore their world, so the Control Room was operated by our *Exploration* team. Those were fascinating years. As the external world became better understood, eventually man turned inward, and the *Age of Enlightenment* held sway over humanity, and our team reflected that change here in the Control Room. Those guys actually referred to themselves as the 'Gods of Enlightenment.' I will admit it has a certain cachet to it. Don't you think? Eventually, that led to our friends Milton, Henry, and Randolph and the era of *Industry and*

Commerce. In each instance, our teams did their job and fostered the belief system they had were assigned—as will we. We are the keepers, the protectors, the guardians, and promoters of *Science and the Scientific Method.* Does that get you up to speed?"

Seymour nodded. "You tell it much more succinctly then they did during orientation. I think they spent a whole day on that."

"How would you know? You were day-dreaming," laughed Marie.

"Well, I, ah, ah, . . ."

"Never mind," said Marie. "Now that you better understand the historical context, let's get back to work."

The team worked, and as they did the belief in science continued to grow. Time passed down on Earth. The team was deft and precise in their manipulations. Certain scientific discoveries led to the rise in mass communications, which was only natural. But then Marie, Felix and even Seymour noticed some irregularities in the Perception and Conviction displays.

They tried to fine tune their adjustments, but to no avail. With the advent of mass communication, humans started to build global networks and eventually social media was on the rise. The pace of change was quickening, almost exponentially. The Perception and Conviction displays began to register a surge in what could be called the "Cult of Personality." They were not allowed to take actions against this shift but were only allowed to foster a belief in their own cause of science.

Marie finally turned to Felix and Seymour, "Gentlemen, we have done some great work, but these humans are a fickle bunch and I believe that science as the ruling belief system is beginning to fade. Far too quickly in my opinion, but there it is"

"They do seem to be inclined towards this *Age of the Individual and Personal Popularity.* I think it is ridiculous," said Felix. They all nodded soberly.

Eventually, Marie spoke for all of them, "We have done all we can do. Our time has not been long here in the Control Room, but I think we can all see how this is going to play out."

She paused, looking down at her tablet display, "In point of fact, I just received a communication from *Management,* another team is on its way. Our time is coming to end. God help them."

Introduction to
He Doesn't Have a Prayer

We tend to think of death in some abstract way. It won't happen to me—at least not yet. If we do think about it, we tend to put a glossy film in our perceptual cameras and think we will be looking down from heaven at our own funeral. How else to explain Facebook posts to our departed loved ones? Do we really think they are reading Facebook in the afterlife—assuming there is an afterlife? News flash folks—death is kind of like a real thing. Everyone who has ever lived has died. Really, no exceptions to date.

"All life is only a set of pictures in the brain, among which there is no difference betwixt those born of real things and those born of inward dreamings, and no cause to value the one above the other."
—H.P. Lovecraft

He Doesn't Have a Prayer

He tossed and turned but sleep, like a locked door for which he did not have the key, would not come. He could pound at the door but what good would that do? So, he lay quietly and stared at the ceiling. There was nothing else he could do.

Ethan hated going to bed. His parents insisted that he get to bed by ten o'clock on school nights. He was twelve and had to get up for school at seven in the morning, so that bedtime made sense, even if sleep eluded him—like grasping a swirling vapor. He would lie awake and think about his own death. His death plagued him, and he didn't know why. There was no rational reason why he should be so consumed by his own fate. But he was. God knows he was.

He wasn't sure when it started. It may have been about six months ago. But again, the why of it all was just not apparent to him. No one close to him had died, not even a family pet. But, he lay in bed night after night with death suspended above him like a suffocating cloud. Unlike other kids his age or even adults he knew, Ethan felt he really understood death. He could feel it; it had definable features to him. He could touch it, and it felt cold. It sent a chill down his spine and into his very soul every time he made contact. He could feel the eternal nothingness stretching out to infinity before him. An eternity going on and on without him because he was going to die. He was going to cease to exist. There was nothing after this. No feathery clouds, no angels, no heaven. How ridiculous that all seemed to him. You lived, and you died. That same process had been going on for a very long time, and he was just one more person in the human menagerie that would come and go.

Ethan threw off the sheets and sat up in his bed. This was driving him nuts. It was so frustrating to try to fall asleep while his mind bounced and hopped around like an unbalanced washing machine. Every time his mind calmed down just a bit, the icy hands of death grabbed hold of him, and he was wide awake and frozen in terror. He needed this to end. Out of desperation, rather than any real sense of belief, he knelt by his bed and prayed. He didn't really believe in God, but he was out of ideas and his mind was in a panic.

He prayed to a God or Gods he didn't really believe in, understand or know, but he did it anyway. He said aloud to the eternal nothingness, "God help me. I don't want to die. I know this is ridiculous, but I can't stop thinking about it. I just can't. I'm just a kid, but even I know that this will all end. Why doesn't anyone else seem to notice? How do they simply ignore their own mortality? I'm here and I'm asking. Don't let me die."

He had no more words he could say. He sighed and climbed back into bed. It was a waste of time and energy, he knew that, but it felt good to unburden himself, at least for a few minutes. Ethan closed his eyes and tried to sleep.

The maniac in the closet smiled. *That was a very nice prayer*, he thought. *Really very nice indeed.* Slowly, with almost imperceptible movements, he reached into his pocket and took out his knife.

Introduction to
Moving on From Nowhere

This story originated in my wife Valerie's fertile imagination. She wanted to explore what happens when a conflict extends past what we normally consider to be the end of our time here on earth. She asked me to take the helm, as it were, of this idea and see if I could bring it to life. I agreed. However, the story was further propelled by a news story in the *Washington Post*, "Teen killed by attacker in robbery attempt." This story attempts to interconnect Val's original idea and the tragic events depicted in the *Washington Post* headline. We may never know what lies beyond, but this story offers one possibility in the land of "What If."

"Deep in the human unconscious is a pervasive need for a logical universe that makes sense. But the real universe is always one step beyond logic."
—Frank Herbert, Dune

Moving on From Nowhere

Part 1: Nowhere

Zachari woke up and remembered dying. At least he assumed he was dead. He remembered the knife going into his side and then into his chest and then the light fading out as he slid into nothingness. He remembered it clearly, but that memory left him confused as to where he was now and more importantly, why he was at all.

He was lying on the ground, around him was a featureless horizon. He arose slowly expecting to feel pain from the stab wounds, but curiously there was none. In fact, as he lifted his shirt, there were no wounds at all. He tried to make sense of his surroundings. He could see in front of him for several yards, although there was absolutely nothing to see. After a few yards, a mist seemed to descend, and he couldn't see anything—no matter the direction.

Part 2: Then

He stood there not knowing exactly what to do as the memory of his death seeped slowly back into his consciousness. He had been coming home from school and had been attacked just blocks from his Washington D.C. home. Zachari attended the University of the District of Columbia in the evenings. He was a freshman in his first semester. During the day, he worked in the cafeteria of the Natural History Museum. It was a lousy job, but the museum itself was a fascinating place to work, and his salary helped pay for some of the college expenses. His parents were paying the lion's share of the bills, and to defray expenses he still lived at home with them in southeast

Washington. He could, in fact, almost see his house when the attack came suddenly from behind.

It had been a cool evening as Zachari had walked up the steps from the Metro station. His house was only a mile or so from the Metro and Zachari could feel a breeze trickling down the steps to the underground subway station. Each step upwards brought the breeze closer to him. He reached the top of the stairs and took in a deep breath of the cool evening air. It was pleasant compared to the stale, manufactured air down in the station. The walk home was pleasant enough at least until he felt a hand grab him from behind and spin him roughly around.

Zachari stumbled as he turned. Regaining his balance, he looked up and saw a man in a grey colored sweat jacket. The man was holding a knife and pointing it at Zachari. Zachari stared in disbelief at the blade. It was large and menacing.

Zachari had grown up in D.C., and while street violence was not uncommon in the city, Zachari had been fortunate; he had never been touched by the violence that had impacted so many of his friends and classmates over the years. Now his luck was about to end.

The man standing in front of him looked at Zachari and he could see the fear in Zachari's eyes. He smiled, "OK, camel boy, hold it right there. You know the score, hand over your cash, your phone, and that fucking backpack while you're at it." He said this without anger but as a simple statement of fact. He said it as if they needed to conduct a business transaction and he was impatient wanting to get the deal done quickly.

"I'm not giving you shit, man," Zachari said. He had meant for it to come out in a deep voice. He had meant it to sound intimidating. He had meant it to sound threatening. It didn't. Instead, what came out sounded like an unsteady whisper. It was as if all the air had been sucked out of his lungs before he uttered a sound.

The man's smiled faded quickly, his face transforming into annoyance and frustration. "Don't do some stupid shit kid. Just hand it all over and do it now. I ain't got no time for some fucking hero bullshit!"

Zachari's bravado began to fade but he couldn't just hand everything over to this asshole. He didn't have a ton of cash, and what he did have, he needed. Plus, he wasn't giving up his backpack. It had all his text books and notebooks inside. Screw that!

Zachari looked around, hoping to find a means of escape or someone to help him. The would-be robber gave a little laugh. "Man, ain't no one around. I've been walking behind you and watching you since you left the Metro. You think I'm some kind of fool?"

He was right, there was no one in sight. The street was empty, and it was now dark, as evening had changed into night since he left the subway station. Zachari took a half step backwards, keeping eye contact with his assailant.

The man stared at Zachari and said impatiently, "Don't even think about it."

Zachari was scared, but he was also pissed. Why the fuck was this happening to him? He was just a couple blocks from his home. So damn close. It was just fucking unfair. Then out of nowhere he heard himself say, "No."

Zachari didn't even realize he was speaking. It was as if someone else was operating his mouth, but the word was out there. A single defiant statement and it hung in the air between them.

"What the fuck did you just say, kid?"

"I said no," Zachari said it again and this time he said it with intention.

The robber made an audible sigh. His body sagged a little, and then he stiffened. A second or two passed. They were both frozen in that instant. Something or someone was going to give. A decision had to be made. A line was going to be crossed.

The thief's eyes hardened, and then he seemed to lunge forward with the blade extended. Zachari didn't have a chance to move. The lunge caught him off-guard. He was expecting more of a signal that the conversation (such as it was) had ended. He was expecting something but not the sudden lunge and the feel of steel sinking into his gut. Oddly there was no immediate sensation of pain—just shock and disbelief.

He heard air rush out from his mouth. He stumbled backward. Instinctively he reached out and tried to grab his assailant, managing to get hold of his jacket. He remembered looking into the man's eyes. He managed to utter one last word. "Why?" he said and then felt the knife pierce his chest.

As he began to fade, he heard the man say, "Kid, didn't have to be like this. Your choice. Your choice."

Part 3: Now

Zachari stood in the meaningless void. The words from his assailant echoed in the stillness. He was still pissed, even as he stood here in this alien landscape. He had been stabbed. For what? A few lousy bucks and a few personal belongings. His life just taken away for almost nothing. His mind then drifted to his parents. They were going to be so upset. This was going to crush them. He wanted to cry but held back the tears. He was not going to let the asshole who had done this have the satisfaction of his tears even if he would never know it.

Wiping his eyes, he once again took in his surroundings. There was nothing in every direction—a formless void. His anger ebbed, and in its place, confusion took hold. He didn't know where he was. He didn't know how he had gotten here. He didn't really know what to do next, but he knew standing there in the nothingness was not much of a plan. He took a few steps and had just reached the misty area that shrouded what lay beyond when he heard a voice from behind him.

"I wouldn't bother. You go out there and you end up back here, no matter which way you go."

Zachari turned around; thirty feet behind him sat a man on the ground. While he could not see him clearly, the man appeared to be slumped with his face looking down at the ground. Zachari hadn't noticed him before. Did he just arrive? If not, why hadn't he seen him until he spoke?

"What do you mean?" Zachari asked.

"I mean exactly what I said." He didn't lift his head as he spoke. "If you don't believe me, go ahead and start walking. In about an hour or so of wandering around in the fog, you'll end up right back here. I've done it a dozen times and each time, well, here the fuck I am."

"How's that possible?" said Zachari.

"Kid, how the fuck should I know?" said the man.

Something about the way he said that last sentence struck Zachari as familiar. "How long have you been here? How did you get here?"

"I have no fucking clue how long I've been here." He said, answering at least one of Zachari's questions.

"What do mean? You must have some idea."

"Do you see a clock on the wall brother? For that matter, do you see a god-damned wall?" He paused. Still looking down, he shrugged. "I really don't know man; time just seems to float on by." He laughed a little as he said it. It was a sorrowful laugh.

Zachari stood there for a moment. Something in the man's voice was familiar all right. And, while Zachari could not exactly say why, he believed the man.

"I'm going anyway. If you're right, I'll see you in an hour. If not, I won't see you at all and I'll be out of here." With that, Zachari started to move into the mist.

"One more thing man. There's some kind of noise out there."

Zachari paused, "What kind of noise?"

"It's hard to describe. It was like a humming sound. Each time I went out there it got louder and louder. I don't know what it is, but I didn't like it. I didn't like it one bit."

"Did you see anything?"

"No, I just heard the sound. Nothing out there that I ever saw."

Zachari considered what he had just heard. It made no sense. None of this made any sense. Somehow, you ended up back at your starting point and there was some indistinct humming sound. Well, this guy came back OK, so the worst that could happen is that he would be back here again. Zachari strode into the mist.

Part 4: Reverse Angle

Jason was tired. He was tired, and he was frustrated. Things had not been going Jason's way this week. In fact, things had not been going Jason's way for a very fucking long time. He was sitting outside the Metro station waiting for an easy target. The sun was about to set, and it would be dark soon and then he could get tonight's shit over with. Ideally, he would find a middle-aged woman who had a purse dangling from her arm. So, he bided his time in a nearby alley and waited. His bad luck continued to hold, and he saw nothing that looked easy. Had all the middle-aged women suddenly left the city? *Well, this just sucks,* he thought.

Jason's patience wore thin and then it wore out. He saw a young kid emerge from the Metro station. He had a backpack and Jason could see the outline of a phone in his pants pocket. It was far from ideal, but if he was going to score anything tonight, it would have to do. Jason started to follow the kid but kept enough space between them so that it did not seem conspicuous. As he walked, Jason wondered why it had to be this way.

Jason's bad luck (as far as he was concerned) had started at birth. For that matter, it had started long before he was even born. His mother was an addict and had gotten pregnant from some guy while she was as high as a fucking kite, so neither she nor Jason would ever know who his father was. Of course, that was just the first course in his banquet of bad luck. While his mother did her best to take care of him, she was basically homeless and had no clue how to care for a newborn. She was not much more than twenty and had no one to help her. Jason's mom had long ago alienated herself from her family. She was entirely on her own.

His mom tried to stay off the drugs and even managed to get a job in a neighborhood grocery store. So, they survived for a time. However, things were far from perfect. Jason wasn't sure if it was her drug use while pregnant or something that happened to him during his first few years, but Jason had some significant learning disabilities, or so they told him when he was old enough to understand this kind of stuff. He was dyslexic and had various memory related problems. He muddled though school, graduating to the next grade mostly because no one seemed to care enough to help.

But Jason's bad luck just kept on coming. When he was fifteen, he came home from school and his mom was gone. No note, no nothing. She was just gone, and she never came back. Perhaps she just couldn't deal with it anymore. Perhaps she went back to using. Jason would never know.

However, Jason did know, even with disabilities, that someone was going to find out that he was all alone, and he would go into the foster care system. He also knew that nobody was going to want a fifteen-year-old kid with learning disabilities. He was going to sit in some foster care facility with a bunch of people who didn't give a shit about him and wait until they kicked him out at age eighteen. Well, he would beat them to the punch and go out on his own now.

Jason eventually made his way down to Washington D.C. from his home in Oxon Hill, Maryland. He got by with odd jobs here and there when he could get them. But since he couldn't read well, there was little he was qualified to do. He started stealing, and he found out he was actually good at it. He had finally found something that would enable him to achieve some modest success. Granted, stealing was against the law, but when your choices are limited, you take what you can get. If he was careful, he could make a decent score here and there and no one got hurt. Yeah, people got scared, but they got to walk away and go back to their cushy lives. As far as Jason was concerned, it was no harm, no foul.

Jason had been on the streets for fifteen years now, and while his life was far from great, he was surviving. Given his past, he was okay with that. A cool wind crossed his face and snapped him out of his reverie. Without even noticing it, he had begun to quicken his pace to catch up to the young kid in front of him.

Again, Jason wished he had an easier target for tonight, but this kid would have to do. Hopefully he had a good phone Jason could pawn and something decent in that backpack. *Be smart*, he told himself. The key was to catch them off-guard and the rest usually followed well enough. Jason pulled out his knife. It was his way of intimidating his mark, and fortunately, he had never had to use it. He reached out and spun the kid around.

Jason and the kid exchanged some back and forth. The exact words, to Jason, were less important than the fact that this kid was not giving up his stuff. Did he not see the six-inch blade in front of him? Why the fuck was he putting up such a stink over a lousy phone, a backpack, and whatever small bills he had in his wallet?

Jason decided the conversation had to end. He needed to make this score and get the heck out of here. Talking on the street was only going to draw attention. He decided to scare the shit out of the kid and so he leaned in with the blade to let the kid see how deadly this knife was up close. As he leaned forward, he lost his balance just slightly and he fell. The blade went straight into the kid's stomach. *Shit*, Jason thought. *Now I've fucking done it.* The kid was bleeding like a fucking pig. *I am screwed so fucking hard.*

He could run, but if he got caught, he would go to prison for a very long time. He glanced down at the kid for a second and could see that he was in bad shape. He didn't think the kid was going to make it. It was going to be a slow painful death. Jason stabbed him again, this time on purpose. He put the blade right into his heart. *End it now*, he thought.

He heard the kid whisper something to him with his last breath. It sounded like the kid said "Why?"

Why? Jason thought. *Why? Because you would just not give up the stupid-ass backpack and phone, you dumb son-of-a-bitch—that's why.* But he didn't say that. He said very simply, "Kid, didn't have to be like this. Your choice. Your choice."

Jason was freaked out. This had never happened before. Nothing even close. He pulled the kid's backpack off. Reaching into the kid's back pocket, Jason pulled out the kid's phone and wallet, and then he darted across the street.

He was so panicked that he never saw the Metro bus coming down the street. The bus driver, for his part, never saw Jason, at least not until it was too late.

Part 5: Know-where

Zachari drifted in the mist. He attempted to keep some semblance of a straight path, but it was impossible to know for sure. For the first few minutes, he kept his hands out in front of him, afraid he would run into a wall or some other obstacle. But, after a while his hands came down. There was nothing out there in the mist to run into. The other guy had been right.

Then he paused. He heard it—the humming sound. It was barely perceptible, like something just out of reach but nevertheless right in front of him. The air seemed to be vibrating as well. The guy never mentioned that. It was disquieting and unnerving.

He stopped trying to navigate a straight path, quickened his pace and just hoped he would find his way back to his starting point. At least he would be out of the mist, away from that noise, and have someone to talk to.

A short time later the mist began to dissipate, and he found himself back at his starting point. His companion in this netherworld was still sitting where he had left him. His head was still down. His body still slouched in a posture that told you more about his state of mind than mere words would ever do—complete and utter resignation.

"You're back," was all he said.

Zachari sat down across from him. "Yeah, I'm back. It's the same in every direction, right?"

"Yes. At least as far as I can tell."

"I heard the noise. At least I think I did. It was weird and yeah, I didn't like it either. So, now what do we do? Zachari asked.

"We?" the man replied. "I didn't know we were a couple."

"I just figured two heads are better than one. By the way, my name is Zachari. Also, I think we're dead."

"No shit man," he said, still not giving up his name.

"Great, so we're both dead, but, where are we?" said Zachari. The man said nothing. Zachari waited and still, the man offered nothing. Finally, Zachari asked the obvious question. "So, how did you die?"

"Got hit by a bus." The man said.

"That sucks." Zachari said and meant it.

"I guess," the man said. "I really don't remember much. I was trying to cross the street and the fucking Metro bus plowed into me."

"Metro bus? You from D.C.?"

"Yeah," he said and then added, "Born in Maryland but came down to D.C. about ten years ago or so."

"I'm from D.C. as well. I went to school there."

"A big fucking congrats to you kid. Guess you're not going to school there anymore."

Zachari paused. There it was again. This guy just sounded so damned familiar. They both lived in D.C., so it was possible they had run into one another before, but the guy seemed like a bit of jerk. Zachari decided to give it one more try.

"I was killed in D.C. A guy tried to rob me and ended up stabbing me twice."

The man didn't reply but his body seemed to tense up. Slowly he raised his head and said, "Wish it didn't have to be like this, kid."

Part 6: Now (Again)

"You!" That was all Zachari could say. He sat frozen. It was him. His attacker was sitting right in front of him. Could his life, or in this case his death, get any stranger? He took a moment to try and process this improbable train of events. First, he's stabbed a few blocks from his home. Then, he wakes up in this crazy place unharmed but feeling slightly unhinged. Now, he finds out that he is stuck in this crazy place with the guy who killed him. Finally, he just blurted out the obvious.

"You fucking stabbed me. I'm here because of you!"

Jason met Zachari's gaze. "Same here kid. If it wasn't for you, I wouldn't be here neither."

"How the heck can you say that with a straight face? I was simply walking home, and you attacked me."

"Kid, all you had to do was hand over your stuff, and we'd both be home now instead of here in Fucked-Up-Land."

"Just hold on a second, asshole. There is no way this is my fault. Your logic is as crazy as this place," he said gesturing to their surroundings. "Also, stop calling me kid. My name is Zachari. Got that?"

Jason sat there for a few seconds. "Fine. Your name is Zachari. What does it matter, especially in this crazy place? My name was Jason, for whatever that's worth."

"So, why'd you do it?" Zachari asked.

"Do what?" Jason countered sounding annoyed.

"Rob me, kill me, take your pick."

"Look, I didn't want to rob you" Jason began but Zachari, cut him off.

"What do you mean you didn't want to rob me? You came right up to me with a knife!"

"Let me finish will ya!" Jason yelled back. Zachari folded his arms and waited. Seeing that he wasn't going to interrupt, Jason continued.

"As I said, I didn't want to rob you, I wanted to find a middle-aged woman with a purse dangling from her arm, but no one fit that description, so you were it. Luck of the draw buddy." Jason knew that would not satisfy this guy, but it was the truth.

As if on cue, Zachari barked back at him. "That's your excuse? I wasn't the best target but what the hell, I was good enough?"

"Look man, I ain't apologizing for nothing. You were there, I needed a score. If you had handed things over, like I said before, we'd be all square and we'd be in a much happier place right now."

Zachari thought this was the most ludicrous logic he'd ever heard. He got up and paced back and forth. He waited and tried to calm down. "You don't get it. Robbing me or anyone else is wrong. Period. You were wrong. Besides, the robbery is just the icing on the cake. You stabbed me. You killed me, and by the way, I'm glad you got hit by a bus!"

"It was an accident," said Jason.

Zachari was once again perplexed and annoyed by his response. "How can you say it was an accident? You drove that knife right into my gut!"

"I didn't mean to do that part. I leaned in to scare you and kind of fell forward and the knife just kind of went into you." Jason stopped talking after that. He really thought that no matter what he said, this Zachari guy was never going to be satisfied.

Zachari glowered at him for a few seconds and was about to yell back when Jason stood up and started walking towards him. Was he about to attack him again? Zachari froze for a second, then put his hands up to fight. But, Jason walked right by him. He stood next to the mist, looking out into its depths. Finally, he said, "I think the mist is closing in on us!"

Zachari turned, and his eyes followed to the area where Jason was staring. He was right, the mist did look as if it had moved closer to them. The open space they were in was definitely smaller than it had been when he had first arrived.

Jason said, "I don't like it. I hate this place, but I don't want to be back in that mist. This is nowhere, but that's really nowhere."

And with that, Jason moved back to where he was before and sat down. Zachari sat down facing Jason. They both just sat there and stared at the mist. After a few moments, the strange humming sound started. Just like before, it seemed just out of reach, but it was definitely there.

Zachari looked at Jason. "Have you ever heard the sound when you were not in the mist?"

"No, only in the mist."

Neither of them said a word but they both could feel each other's nervousness. Zachari's mind wandered back to the stabbing. Could Jason's act of stabbing him have been an accident? Was it possible? The final events had happened quickly. They had been talking and suddenly the knife was in his stomach. The whole fucking thing was a confusing nightmare.

Zachari looked at Jason, "Was I the first?"

Lost in his own thoughts, Jason looked up. "What?"

"Was I the first person you ever killed?"

"You're the first person I ever had to stab. So yes, you were the first." Jason paused and gathered his thoughts. "Look, I ain't apologizing or anything, but like I said, I didn't mean to stab you. But then the fucking blade was in you, and you were bleeding out. I didn't know what to do, so I stabbed you again. I needed to end it."

Zachari believed him. He had no reason to lie—not in this place, not now. Zachari, wasn't sure what to do with that information. It didn't change anything, at least he didn't think so.

"So, you stabbed me and then got hit by a bus?"

"About ten seconds later."

"Then how come you ended up here before I did?"

"I have no fucking clue, kid, um, I mean Zachari. I have no clue. Everything seems out of joint here."

"Yeah, you got that right," replied Zachari.

They sat in silence for some time. At some point, Zachari got up and sat beside Jason. As he did, he noticed that the humming sound was now gone. It seemed to have dissipated as they talked. Zachari mentioned this as they sat together. Jason nodded and a slight smile slid across his face.

Part 7: Moving Forward

Nothing happened for a long time. At least it felt like a long time to Jason and Zachari. They eventually started to talk about other things. They talked about their lives. They talked about their likes and dislikes. They talked about all manner of things because here in this Nowhere Land there was nothing else to do but talk. It was the only thing that held off the despair and the loneliness. They eventually found a few things they had in common but found more things that were alien and strange to each other. But they continued to talk.

At some point, Zachari happened to look up. He stared at the mist. It looked as if the mist had receded. He turned to Jason. "Do you see that?"

"If you're talking about the mist. Yep, I think I do. It looks to be fading a bit."

Zachari got up and moved towards the mist. Nothing happened. It did not recede nor did it advance. Jason got up and joined him at the perimeter. The mist then receded a bit.

"Did you see that?" Zachari said, knowing that Jason must have seen it, but feeling a need to say something anyway.

"I sure as shit did see that!"

"Let me try an experiment," said Zachari.

"Go ahead college boy," replied Jason.

Zachari moved a few steps to his left and then headed over to the mist. The mist held and did not move. Zachari, then moved back over to Jason. He grabbed his hand. At first Jason started to pull his hand away, but then he let Zachari take hold. It felt odd to hold hands, but he wanted to see how this was going to play out. Zachari gently moved them over to the left and approached the mist. It receded! It seemed to have no interest in them if they stood side-by-side.

They stood there for a few minutes, both seeming to understand what was happening. If they were going to leave this place, they were going to have to go together. They could not say for sure what lay ahead, but they understood that they were being allowed to move on from this place of nothingness. However, there was an entrance fee—only by laying aside their anger, their pain, and their limited perspective could they move on to something beyond this possibility.

So, Zachari and Jason left this place where time and space seemed not to matter. They were not friends, but they had begun down a path to understanding and that was enough. It was just enough in this Nowhere Land.

Introduction to
What's On the Menu?

Time to pull out the big guns. I am going to tread on some sacred ground here, but as the old saying goes—no risk, no reward. I know that many storytellers have gone to similar places, but here's my take on the universe, free will, and the mysteries that surround us all. As I said, it is sacred ground, however, it is also fertile soil to shape and twist our reality into forms that resemble our world but move into unknown territory when we least expect it.

"Reality is that part of the imagination we all agree on."
—Unknown

What's On the Menu?

The headlights emanating from Ben's SUV struck the fog and died there. Ben could see perhaps fifty yards in front of him, but no more. He had been driving for almost two hours in these miserable conditions and needed a break; he was tired, and his eyes hurt from the continued strain. He never should have left the beach house in the first place, but business was business, and the meeting was urgent if his company was going to seal the deal on their latest potential property. Ben's company wanted to build an upscale office park in Alameda, which was near enough to San Francisco to be desirable, but not so far as to be inexpensive. It was what his boss called a "Goldilocks" property. Ben had been on vacation with his family when the meeting got scheduled, but what could he do? Life didn't just stop because he and his family were on vacation.

Ben knew he was going to get an earful when he got back to the beach house. He had promised Ana that he would be gone no more than an hour, and she had grudgingly agreed. He neglected to emphasize the fact that he would need to drive two and half hours each way to make the meeting. So, basically the day was shot. Add to that, the meeting lasted three hours, and now this blasted fog had rolled in from nowhere. He knew that his return to the house was going to be as unpleasant as the weather now surrounding him.

Am I lost? Ben thought. No, he had not diverted from the route provided by the car's GPS and this had him headed straight for the coast, though nothing looked familiar. Of course, he couldn't see much, thanks to good old Mr. Fog out there, but he was worried nonetheless.

Suddenly, cutting through the fog like a laser was a bright red and yellow sign on his right. It seemed to simply burn the fog away. The sign read "Gino's Diner." Ben considered, "What the hell?" he said. "I could use a break; I'll grab a cup of coffee and something to eat. Besides, the fog might lift if I give it some time. It's going to make me even later, but I can call Ana from the diner and explain."

Ben pulled into the parking lot and got out of the car. At the last minute, he remembered to grab his cell phone to call Ana but he wasn't getting any reception. "Not one freaking bar!" he exclaimed. "It figures."

Ben entered the restaurant and was greeted with a barren expanse. There was no one in the place. It looked clean and well lit, just empty. Poised in front of the counter were a dozen or so thin shiny stools with red vinyl covers. The floor consisted of alternating black and white tiles. The booths and tables completed the décor, and every aspect was something out of a 1950s diner. Ben recalled sitting down with his father to watch "American Graffiti" when he was a teenager. This place would have fit right into that film.

Ben picked a place at the counter and sat down. Within a few seconds the kitchen doors swung open revealing a man of perhaps sixty, dressed in the customary white smock and apron. He had dark curly hair and the beginnings of a paunch underneath his apron. He wore a thick mustache and had eyebrows to match. *Right out of central casting*, Ben thought. If God was going to design a guy named Gino (and Ben assumed this guy was indeed the Gino identified by the neon sign) this was what he would look like.

"Good evening my friend. Nice of you to stop in. What can I get ya?"

"Kind of dead around here," Ben replied.

"Yeah, we have our ups and downs, but we make do. So, what'll it be?

"Got a menu?"

"Sure, but we serve just about anything. Tell me what you're in the mood for, and I'll bet you we got it, and I'll bet it's the best dish you've ever had."

"Pretty confident about that, eh?" said Ben. The man nodded. "Well if this place is so good, why no customers?" Ben spread his hands out wide, gesturing to the empty restaurant.

"Like I said, traffic comes and goes. Trust me, the food is the least of your issues," he returned Ben's gesture, pointing to the fog outside that had somehow gotten worse in the last few minutes. "The fog is bad this evening. I hope you don't have any place you need to be right away?"

"In fact, I do, but driving in this shit was near impossible and your sign just appeared, like out of nowhere, so I figured a little food and coffee would do me good."

"Well here, let me pour you a cup of joe." The man pulled a pot off the burner and poured Ben a cup. Ben took a sip.

"Damn, that is good. If your food is as good as the coffee, then I guess I won't take your bet. By the way, you wouldn't happen to have a landline here? I need to call my wife and the cell reception here is for shit."

"Nope, sorry no landline, and the cell reception is pretty much nonexistent here. Apologies about that. But since the fog is so bad and you're here, have something to eat, and we'll see if the weather clears up."

"OK," Ben agreed. "Might as well have something to eat. Any recommendations, since you seem to be short on menus?"

"Oh, I got a menu but don't worry about that. I'll show it to you later. But seriously, everything here is good. Just name it."

"OK, give me some chicken parmesan," Ben said. He figured with a name like Gino, an Italian dish seemed only appropriate.

"You got it my man. I'll go back and place the order. Be right back."

He ducked through the doors into what Ben presumed was the kitchen and came back a minute later. "Your food will be up shortly. By the way, the name's Gino, like it says on the sign. What's yours?"

"I kind of figured you were Gino," said Ben. Gino smiled in return. "My name is Ben. Ben Stairs."

"A pleasure Ben. So, what's your deal? Where are you headed?"

"I was headed home when this Godforsaken fog set in."

Gino just stared at Ben. "When I asked where you were headed, I didn't just mean tonight." Gino said, a wry smile crossing his face, but slightly hidden beneath the bushy mustache.

Ben stared back at Gino, not sure what to make of that statement. "Um, come again?"

"I think you heard me clear enough." He held up a finger, "But hold that thought for a moment. I smell chicken parmesan and it smells good to me. Be right back." With that, he once again slid into the kitchen. He popped back out within seconds carrying a steaming plate.

Ben took in the smell. *Wow*, he thought. Gino was right, it smelled delicious. Distracted by the food, Ben almost forgot Gino's perplexing comment. He dug into his food and tried to forget everything else. He gobbled down a few bites and looked up. Gino was smiling down at him. "Told you," he said. "Is that the best chicken parm you've ever had, or what?"

Ben took the napkin from the counter and wiped some tomato sauce from his chin. "You weren't kidding. Compliments to the chef."

"Would you like to tell him in person?" Gino said pointing to the double doors that led to the kitchen. "Come on," he continued, "It will only take a second, and I'm sure it will be worth it."

Ben considered the offer. This was getting a tad weird, but what the hell? A quick thank you to the chef—what could be the harm? Ben got up slowly, walked around the counter, and followed Gino to the kitchen doors. Gino made an exaggerated gesture that signaled Ben to go first. Slowly, Ben pushed open the doors and peered into the next room. It took a moment for his eyes to adjust and a second or two longer for his brain to make sense of what he was seeing. Or to be more specific—what he wasn't seeing. There was no kitchen behind the doors. There was nothing behind the doors. Ben started to pull back. In front of him was nothing but a gray expanse. There was just nothing there. It was not the gray of the fog outside; no, it was deeper than that. His stomach dropped because deep in the back of his brain, he sensed that he was looking at an eternity of nothingness.

He pulled all the way back into the diner and stumbled back around the counter to his chair. He looked around; everything appeared normal. The chair, the counter, the fucking diner appeared normal. It was all there.

Gino had followed him back into the diner. "Take a deep breath there Ben. Just breathe. You'll be fine in a minute."

"What the fuck was that?" he said finally. "What the hell was I seeing? Change that. What was I not seeing? Why was there nothing there? Where the fuck is your kitchen? Where's the rest of the diner? What the hell is going on here?"

"Easy there Ben, you're going to blow a gasket. Like I said, just breathe."

Ben did as Gino suggested. He tried to calm himself. He took in some deep breaths. Then, absently, he started to eat the chicken parmesan. He wasn't hungry now, he wasn't even thinking about food, but his subconscious mind yearned for normalcy and eating fit the bill. So, he ate.

"OK, I get it. You're a tad freaked out. I get that, but I can explain this if you're willing to listen."

Ben nodded. What else could he do? This was beyond anything he could comprehend. Perhaps this was some weird ass reality TV show and there was some rational explanation here. Gino didn't look like David Copperfield, but maybe this was some kind of crazy magician's trick. He was ready to accept just about any explanation.

"Good," said Gino. "Let's begin with some basics. This diner doesn't really exist in your space-time. It exists someplace entirely different. It resides in what your scientists might call n- dimensional space, although in this case, that is just an approximation. I guided you here, so we could have a chance to talk."

"I have no fucking clue what you just said, but go on. At least nothing is disappearing while you're talking."

"I won't bore you with the mathematical details, but suffice it to say, we are having this conversation in a real diner, just not in a dimension you normally perceive."

Ben nodded again though he was still not entirely sure he understood. "So why am I here? What do you want with me? Are you some kind of alien?"

"Let me address the last question first. No, I am not an alien, at least not in the way you think about these things. Secondly, I guided you here just to talk. Nothing bad will happen to you here, I guarantee that. In fact, you are safer here than on the road out there. Nothing can harm you here, and you won't be here too long in any event. After we've had a chance to chat, you can go on your merry way. Sound good?"

"Fine, I guess. But, that doesn't really explain much."

"Good," said Gino. I noticed that while we've been talking you managed to finish the chicken. Care for some dessert?"

Ben was beginning to think this guy or whatever he might be was absolutely nuts. "No, I don't want dessert. Jeez, can we just get on with it? Whatever *it* is."

"We *are* getting on with it, Ben. Look at that menu you asked about awhile back and see if there is anything you like." Gino handed Ben a menu. Ben, exasperated, took the menu from Gino and opened it up. At the top were some dessert choices—cheese cake, pecan pie, apple pie, in short, the usual stuff. "Fine, I'll take some apple pie. Happy?"

"Fine," said Gino. "I'll get that for you." He reached below the counter and pulled out an apple pie, presumably from thin air, or so it seemed to Ben. Gino handed him the pie; it even had a scoop of vanilla ice cream on top.

"But, do me a favor," Gino said, "look down at the rest of the menu." Ben looked from the apple pie back to the menu. He didn't like the way Gino was suddenly pushing the whole menu thing on him, but slowly he opened it back up and looked below the dessert selections. Below the dessert heading was another heading. It simply said **JOB** in big bold letters. Below the heading there were three choices:

- Commercial Real Estate Broker
- Law
- Photography

Ben looked at the choices a second time. Understanding crept softly into his mind, like a gentle breeze. He had been in commercial real estate for about ten years now after graduating from college. It paid well, but Ben was basically ambivalent about the whole thing. The hours sucked, and his boss, Bill Davenport never seemed to be satisfied. Davenport loved the work—God knows why and was always looking to the next deal and the deal after that.

Below his current job was simply the word "Law." Ben knew why that was on the list. Working in real estate, Ben was always dealing with various legal and contractual matters, and the law and its various intricacies interested him. He had wondered on many occasions if he would be better suited for the law, perhaps criminal law, over his present job.

The last one, photography, practically jumped off the page. He had not taken a real photo in years. Ben was not counting the bullshit pictures he took on his iPhone; no, he was thinking about the pictures he used to take on his Nikon D3400. That was a camera! Ben remembered how it took him a week to convince Ana to let him buy the thing. It cost a bundle and back then they were still struggling financially. Eventually, she had relented, and Ben had spent the next several months taking pictures like a mad man. But, that was years ago. As time went on, the picture taking hunger passed and pressures from work ate away at his free time. It was also about that time that Ana got pregnant and spare time for taking pictures just faded away. He had been pretty good though, at least he thought so in retrospect. He had even sold one or two pictures to an online magazine.

Ben looked up from the menu. "OK, so you obviously know some stuff about me. Just who the hell are you?"

"I'll make you a deal. I'll tell you who I am, but in return, you tell me something about those menu choices. Deal?"

Ben considered the offer as he ate some of the apple pie. One thing for sure, wherever he was, the food was the best he had ever tasted! It was a stupid thought to pop into his head at that moment, but he couldn't help himself. Chuckling he said, "Damn, this pie is good." Gino just smiled.

"Fine," Ben finally said. He didn't think he had too much choice. "OK, so who the heck are you, and how do you know so much about me?"

"Well, that's actually two questions but my answer will cover both," Gino said, grinning just a bit. "Basically, I am what you refer to as God. I would guess that answers your second question as well. I just know stuff. It comes with the job."

Ben gaped. "Look, this whole thing is way above my pay grade, I get that, but you're not God. I'm pretty darn sure about that."

"Really, four years of college and ten years in commercial real estate, and you're an expert in theology?" Gino paused for effect. "You have a better theory to explain all this?"

"Well n-n-no," Ben stammered "not off the top of my head but look at you. Nothing personal but you don't appear very God-like. You know," said Ben pointing at Gino, "you look so, ah, ethnic. . ." Ben said trailing off, not sure how to finish the sentence—not even sure he should finish the sentence, and pretty sure he shouldn't have started the sentence in the first place.

"Offense taken!" Gino thundered, and his voice rumbled through the diner like a herd of rhinos. Ben recoiled at the noise. He suddenly felt scared. Then, Gino smiled. "Just messing with you kid. In all honesty, I don't really have a physical form and the particular masque you see before you just seemed appropriate given the surroundings. I can appear with any face or form you like." With that his face dissolved into an opaque, blank slate and then, that space began to spin like a slot machine, hundreds of faces flashed before Ben's eyes in seconds. It was impossible to focus on any one face as they went by too quickly. Eventually the spinning slowed and stopped back to Gino's face.

Ben sat there dumbfounded. He had no words, no thoughts, no way to comprehend what he had just seen. Did he really see that? *Perhaps*, he thought, *if I close my eyes and just pretend I am still in my car this will all go away.* He closed his eyes. He waited. He opened them. No change; same diner, same mustached owner, same fog outside, same sanity melting away like the vanilla ice cream that sat on his apple pie.

"You get the point. I was thinking of doing a George Burns face like in the movie *Oh God*, but it was a little before your time and seemed a tad trite. Don't you think?"

"Who's George Burns?" Ben managed to get out.

"Exactly," said Gino.

Ben waited. After a time, he said, "I guess you're God or something. I don't know what to make of any of this."

"Fair enough," said Gino. "So, I answered your questions satisfactorily?"

"Yeah, sure. I'm good. But, no more spinning faces, OK?"

"Agreed. So, let's get back to the whole job question, shall we? You have been working in commercial real estate for a decade. The question on the table is —is that really what you want to do?"

"Why don't you tell me? You know everything," replied Ben.

"Ben, my boy, it doesn't work like that. You have free will, and you make the choices."

Ben considered Gino's question. His brow furrowed as he thought. He just didn't know. Gino let him think for a few minutes and busied himself with cleaning the dishes from the counter. Gino then looked back at Ben who was obviously struggling with the question.

"Sometimes it helps to talk it over out loud. Let me be a sounding board for you," Gino said.

"It's not an easy question to answer," replied Ben. "By the way, why do I need to decide this now?"

"You don't have to decide this minute, but you are at a crucial point in your life and the decisions you make in the next weeks and months will determine the course of your life. That's why I'm here."

"Shouldn't you be off running the universe or something? Besides, why me?"

"You are full of questions," responded Gino. "But, the short answer is that no one is running the universe, at least not in the way you framed the question. As to why you? Why not you? Look, the way this whole thing works is that I can engage in a limitless number of these conversations at the same time. I like you, so we are having a little conversation. Got it?"

Ben nodded in agreement and then after a moment shook his head no. He wasn't sure what he understood. He paused and then said, "So you're not in charge of the universe?"

Gino sighed, "This gets a little complicated. You're sure you would be happy with the old 'I am that I am' routine? I mean I didn't write that line, but it kind of sums things up nicely."

"No," Ben said, "that really doesn't tell me all that much."

"I get ya. I get ya." said Gino. "Personally, I try not to think about it much. I'm not that into self-reflection. The whole thing can give you a headache. But, I'll do my best to explain. First, regarding me, and I hate to use that pronoun here, but it will do for now. It might be best to think of me as a noun, a verb, and an adjective. I can see that brow of yours furrowing again, so just hold on for a minute there Benjamin. I am, in fact, all three at the same time. If you think of me as a noun, then quite simply, I am the universe. I am the whole gosh darn thing. The universe, heck, the multi-verse and I are one and the same. So, I am not exactly running it, I am it."

He waited, giving Ben a chance to digest this, which would probably be a lot harder to get down than the chicken parmesan and apple pie.

"Think of it this way," he continued, "there are some one hundred trillion cells in the human body. Do you actively control each cell's movements and purpose?"

"Well no," said Ben. "Wait . . . I have one hundred trillion cells inside me?"

"Give or take a few million, yes. These cells work according to the plan of the body supporting life. In this case, your life. You are not actively controlling the work of these individual cells but each one, and the activities they perform, make up the Ben Stairs sitting in front of me now. In the same way, all the beings and activity in the universe are me and it all runs according to a predefined set of rules or laws. I don't control, manage, or run it. I am it. And the laws guiding and governing the universe, like gravity and electro magnetism, are also me. These never-ending processes are the verbs, and I am all of them. I am the process."

Ben interrupted, "I'm pretty sure gravity is a noun, not a verb."

"First, you're an expert in theology and now you're an English major!" Gino laughed. "Technically speaking you're right, but I'm referring to all the activities taking place every millisecond based on these laws, and so when an object falls—notice that the word *falls* is a verb—I am the causal agent behind that activity. I am gravity. I cause the object to fall. Happy?"

Ben nodded. "Go on."

"Deists like to think of me as the master clock maker," he continued. "And, they are right in some respects. They believe that I made the universe and set it in motion, like that clock on the wall," he said pointing to the far wall of the diner. "Deists theorize that I created the universe and just let that clock tick-tock away. That's not a bad analogy as far it goes. Generally speaking, I don't meddle in human affairs. I might be a master clock maker, to overuse their analogy, but I would make a shitty repairman. But here is where the analogy falls short. I am not separate and apart from the clock on the wall or in this case the universe, I am the universe and the process by which it works, all at the same time."

Gino stopped there for a moment to assess Ben's comprehension. He looked like he was trying to figure out Einstein's *Theory of Relativity* without the benefit of ever having taken a math class. "I know. I told you it could give you a headache. That's why I try not to think about it."

"You said you were a noun, a verb, and an adjective. So, what's the adjective?" Ben asked.

"Good question but let me turn that back on you. What adjective would you give it?"

"Incomprehensible!" exclaimed Ben.

"You're not alone in that assessment. Some have called it mysterious. Some call it majestic. The adjective is in the eye of the beholder. At any precise moment, your description of the totality of everything might change. But, like the sky, it's ever changing, but always perfect."

Ben looked at Gino, "Ever changing and always perfect. Sounds like some silly Facebook post or a Hallmark card."

Gino shrugged, "A little over the top for your taste? Too schmaltzy?"

"Yeah, a touch," Ben replied with a smirk. He was beginning to enjoy this crazy-ass conversation. The whole thought of having a conversation with God (however you defined it) still freaked him out, but if he just thought of it as a conversation with a guy named Gino, it was easier to swallow, and he supposed that was the whole point.

"So, Ben, now that we've delved into the depths of theology and the wonders of the universe—which are the same thing as you now know—let's get back to more earthly matters, namely what do you want to do? How do you feel about the menu choices?"

"I'm not really sure. Are you suggesting I need to switch careers right this second?"

"Not at all, but your question reveals an underlying decision that your subconscious has apparently already made while we have been discussing the universe and my existence," said Gino.

"What's that?"

"Well, obviously that you want to change careers!"

"Oh, I guess you're right." Ben said with some dawning enlightenment. "I guess I do want to really try photography, but I am not sure I can make a real living at that. At least, not at nearly the same salary as I make now. I think I would need to make a slow transition as I save some cash."

"Now you're doing it. This isn't like some silly made for TV movie. You don't suddenly decide I am a photographer and poof, you're selling million-dollar pictures. It takes a plan. It takes hard work. It might not even work out," replied Gino.

"Now hold on there. I'd sure as heck like for it to work out. Can't you do a little magic and make that happen? You know, for a friend." Ben smiled, hoping that Gino might be willing to throw a tiny miracle in his direction.

"Sorry, old boy, I just don't work that way. It sucks, doesn't it? I get that. Here you are talking to the *Cause of All Things* and you don't get even a lousy t-shirt for the effort!" Gino smiled and his moustache turned upwards at the ends, giving his face a slightly mischievous appearance. "Of course," he continued, "if it makes you feel any better, you won't remember the specifics of this conversation after you leave here anyway. All that you'll remember is coming to some realizations along your drive home."

Ben's face drooped precipitously. "Now, don't get all pouty on me," said Gino.

Ben pondered this for a minute and then said, "I guess that makes sense. If I started telling people I talked to God, they'd put me away. Still it would be nice to remember something about this. Stuff like this doesn't happen every day."

"It might happen more than you think," countered Gino. "If you can't recall such a conversation, who's to say this is the first time we've talked?"

Ben's mouth hung open. "Have we spoken before?" Gino made no reply, instead he started wiping the counter with a dish towel and humming quietly to himself. This went on for a minute or two. Ben got the message. He wasn't getting an answer to that question.

"OK, I get it. You can stop humming. You're not that great."

"I'll have you know, I am very musical. I've inspired a lot of music, and I have been told I have a lovely voice."

"Maybe so, but you can't carry a tune," Ben laughed at his jibe.

"To each his own," muttered Gino. "Why don't you look at the menu again?" Gino said extending the menu in Ben's direction.

"Do I have to? I've already made the big decision."

"Are you sure you made the big decision? There might be another item on that menu for you to consider."

The menu hung there in Gino's hand like an unwanted letter from the IRS or an unexpected call from an ex-girlfriend, but eventually Ben took it from Gino's outstretched hand. Ben's trepidation stemmed from some idea of what he might see when he opened the menu. He didn't want to look. He was a practiced avoider of hard choices, which is perhaps why he was here in Gino's restaurant in the first place, and he had a sense of what he might find next. Slowly, he opened it up. The menu no longer had any options related to work and career, instead the heading in bold simply said **Relationship.**

Ben tried to force his eyes not to move down the page. He really didn't want to read what the choices were, but it seemed his eyes had a curiosity all their own, and they drifted down below the heading. There he saw the following on the menu page:

- Ana Stairs
- Denise Walkins
- True Love
- Jennifer Garner

Ben's mind focused for now on the top two names on the list. He wasn't surprised to see his wife Ana's name at the top of the list. He loved Ana, that was real. But, if the truth be told, he wasn't surprised to see Denise's name either. He had been flirting with Denise off and on for three years, and while nothing had ever happened, there was something there. He had met Denise after joining a local softball league where each team represented the company they worked for. Denise worked for a local law firm called Jasnoff and Bratman and Ben had met her during the first game he had ever played in the league. Ben had noticed Denise right off. She was playing third base, and in the fifth inning, he had gotten a single and stole second base. He had then moved to third on a sacrifice fly. He stood on third base, and they both kept stealing glances at each other. The next two batters struck out, so Ben was left stranded at third base for the remainder of the inning. Those strike outs had given him and Denise plenty of time to exchange sideways glances.

It was customary for the teams to grab a beer or two after the game, and that's when Denise struck up a conversation with Ben. "Not much luck scoring today,'" she had said by way of introduction. She had appeared seemingly out of nowhere, and her statement caught Ben off guard. He couldn't do much more than stammer out, "Yeah, no luck at all."

"Perhaps your luck will change," she said and giggled at her sophomoric pick up line. Ben laughed as well. From that point on, they kept up the flirtatious banter. Along the way, they got to know each other well through occasional calls, texts, and meet ups after games. He had to admit he liked her. He liked her a lot.

But there was Ana. He loved her, he told himself. They had a good relationship, and they both loved their daughter Linda. That love for Linda bound them together, like an invisible rope tied around their souls. Slowly, inexorably, Ben's eyes went back to the third item on the list,

True Love. *What was that supposed to mean?*

"Great menu you have in this place," Ben said sardonically. "Remind me never to come back here."

"Don't worry, I don't suspect you'll ever see this place again. Free will can be a bitch sometimes. Sorry about that, but what are you going to do? Gino paused, "I know that last part may have sounded rhetorical, but really, what are you going to do?"

"OK, but what is Jennifer Garner's name doing on the list? I mean, what do I have to do with a famous actress?"

"Actually, nothing. I just threw her name on the list for fun. I have a thing for her. One of the universe's best works, if I do say so myself," he said with a chuckle. "Sorry about that, I couldn't resist. But getting back to the question at hand, what are you going to do?"

Ben smiled grudgingly at Gino's little quip. "I guess lying to you is out of the question?" Ben said with a slight smile.

"A lie to me is a lie to yourself. I mean that literally. Given that I am all things, that therefore includes you. You and I, in a sense, overlap so you might as well speak the truth as much as you know it."

Ben sighed. "This is worse than the career decision by a fucking landslide. I'm guessing you know how I feel about Ana and Denise."

"I do, but why don't you verbalize it all the same?"

"OK, as you know, I love Ana, but marriage is hard. It takes a toll. I'm not sure there is that much spark left in the fire, if you know what I mean." Gino nodded at Ben. "I still love Ana and all, but I wish we didn't argue about stupid shit all the time. I just wish things were easier."

Ben lowered his head and looked at the diner floor. Black and white squares lined the floor, and Ben's eyes danced from one tile to the other. Black or white. Black or white. Eventually, he said, "Denise is special, at least I think she is. How the heck do I make a choice like this in such a messed-up situation—eating in the diner from nowhere, with God watching every move I make?"

"I'd be watching regardless. Remember, you and I overlap. Think of it like a Venn diagram of overlapping circles. The place where the two circles intersect, while not large, is where we connect."

"I don't have enough to deal with and you're throwing algebra at me!"

"Technically, it's more like a combination of logic, statistics, and geometry, but sorry about that. Go on."

"Well, I'm not sure I have too much more to say, but I do have a question."

"You want to know about True Love?"

"Yeah, I guess I do."

"Fair enough. What if I were to tell you that your True Love is still out there? What if I were to tell you that it's not Ana and it's not Denise? Ben looked hard at Gino. Was he messing with Ben? Ben couldn't tell. But, before Ben could speak, Gino continued, "Or, what if I told you that True Love is a bullshit idea? That the whole thing is a myth? What answer feels right to you?"

Ben considered the question, "I guess I would say, that I think it's a myth, but what do I know? Why don't you enlighten me?"

"I'd be happy to, but I am not sure you'll love my answer."

"Do I ever?" responded Ben.

"OK then, the answer is that True Love does exist, but not for everyone. Some people are built in such a way that True Love is a possibility for them. They will meet one person, and that person will fill them completely, that person will be the love of their life. But for others, and you've correctly guessed that you are one of the others, they will never experience True Love. It is just not in the cards for them. You, Ben Stairs, are just not built that way. That doesn't mean you won't fall in love. Heck, you've already done that. But, True Love, the type of love that feeds endorphins a continual diet of happy pills, is just not for you. You're going to have to work a little harder to stay in love."

"Well ain't my life just so much fun," was all Ben could say.

"Now don't get all down in the mouth. You have a loving and caring wife. You have a child that you both love. You have a woman out there named Denise that thinks you're hot stuff. From where I sit, that's not too bad."

"All true, I guess," replied Ben. "But it doesn't necessarily make me feel too much better and doesn't make the menu selection any easier."

"Oh, I think it might. Look, you now know that you're not built for True Love. Right? So, I ask you, given that neither Ana nor Denise are not, technically speaking, your True Love, because you don't have one, who do you want to be with?"

Ben didn't hesitate, "Ana," he said. "Denise is fantastic but take away the fairytale, take away the concept of True Love, and I'll stay with the woman I've been married to for the last twelve years, who loves me, and who is the mother of our child."

Gino smiled. It was the smile of a parent pleased with the progress his son is making when he does his homework. "Good work Ben. Free will isn't always easy, but it has its own rewards."

"I suppose I should say thank you," said Ben.

"No need to thank me, I just asked a question or two. Besides, the real work lies ahead of you."

"I know, I know." Ben stood up and stretched his legs. "I'm thirsty, can I get a drink?"

"Sure," said Gino. "How about a nice lemonade?"

Ben nodded, and Gino went to the fountain and got Ben a glass of lemonade.

Ben took a long sip and considered his situation. Here he was talking to Gino in this strange place, having the strangest conversation, and he really didn't know how to categorize it inside his head. He didn't even know how to think about Gino. He understood what Gino had said before about his nature and the universe, but Ben had been brought up to believe in a personal God—not quite an old man with the flowing white beard but, something more personal than the universe and the forces of nature.

"Gino," he said at last. "Or should I say God? When I leave here, am I supposed to pray to you?"

Gino walked around the counter and sat down in the seat next to Ben. "Remember that when you leave here you won't really remember any of this. Besides you didn't pray all that much before coming here, so I kind of doubt you will do so in the future."

"Don't you know for sure? Don't you know the future?"

"In a sense, I know the future. I can calculate to about the millionth decimal point what you will do based on your makeup, who you have relationships with, your total knowledge base, and your history, but there is that pesky free will thing and that throws an element of uncertainty into things. Plus, there is some quantum uncertainty built into the whole thing to keep it interesting. Hence, there is a tiny margin for error in predicting the future. In either case, I try not to think about the future. I tend to let things happen. I really don't dabble in human affairs much."

"Wait a second there. Didn't you, you know, write the Bible, or at least inspire it?"

"The Bible? Heck no. First, of all I hate to write, and besides, I've had a horrible case of writer's block the last couple million years. I just look at a blank page and I get all anxious. I haven't written much more than a few thousand fortune cookies during all recorded history."

"What? You're telling me that you had nothing to do with the Bible or any religious text?"

"Well, I wouldn't go that far. As I said, I am the guiding force in the universe, so to the extent that I caused the whole thing to begin with, I guess I can take some ownership. But really, the whole religion thing is kind of your invention, not mine. Like I said, I dabbled in some fortune cookies, just for kicks a few years back, but then the big corporations got into it, and I felt like my stuff just didn't fit in. I had some really nifty sayings in those cookies back in the day, but alas, that ended."

Ben just sat there with his mouth wide open. He had incorrectly assumed that even though Gino did not seem to fit into the traditional religious construct he grew up with, that he was still the same God as in the Bible.

"So, there is no personal God, like in the Bible." It wasn't a question, it was a dawning realization on Ben's part. "There is no one to really pray to. There is no one to protect us. There is no one pulling the strings and guiding humanity. That seems rather bleak."

"It is the same universe it has always been. How you perceive it now might be different, but it is still the same place, with the same amount of beauty, love, injustice, and pain as before. If you were expecting a definitive happy ending for all humanity, well I guess then you might be a bit disappointed. If you were expecting some type of prize at the end, I am sorry to disappoint you. No prize at the end. The prize, my friend, is at the beginning."

"If I get your drift, then there is no heaven. No personal God and no afterlife. This will take some getting used to."

"Hey, I am standing right in front of you. That's not personal enough?"

"Sorry, I meant no offense, but you're just a manifestation. It's hard to form a deep, long-lasting relationship with the whole darn universe. You're not a real thing. Again, no offense."

"I am real, but I see the point you are struggling with. While I am not exactly what you grew up believing in, I am real. I am one hundred percent real and I am, at this moment, both man and spirit equally."

"How do you do that?"

"I don't do anything; it is just my nature. Our time here in the diner is coming to an end, but I'll try to explain this via an analogy. There is something in physics called the Double Slit experiment. Let me give you the basics of how it works. Think of marbles being shot by a gun at a wall but there is a sheet of metal with a slit in the middle, between the gun and the wall. Then picture the marbles hitting a wall a few feet further on. The marbles going through the slit would result in line of marbles on the back wall. The same result happens if you have two slits—you would just get two lines on the back wall. Are you with me so far?"

Ben nodded. "First math, now physics. I'm thrilled," he grumbled.

"Bear with me for just a minute or two more. Now, picture the same experiment with water. If you push a wave of water through a single slit, the wave passes through the slit and radiates out to the back wall to form a single mark. But, if you do the experiment with two slits then you get an interference pattern on the back wall as waves passing through the slits interact with each other."

Ben looked confused. Gino frowned and then snapped his fingers. Suddenly, the floor of the diner was awash in water and the experiment materialized before Ben's eyes. Now, he saw the interference pattern. Gino then snapped his fingers again and the water disappeared.

"Now, if we repeat this same experiment with electrons, which can be said to be tiny bits of matter like the marbles, we see something different. If we shoot electrons through a metal sheet with a single slit, we see the same pattern we see with the marbles. Now, one might suppose that if you shot electrons through a metal sheet with two slits you would see two bands of electrons on the back wall. But you don't. With two slits, you get an interference pattern. In essence, the electrons act as both a particle and a wave at the same time. The whole thing is way more complicated than this simple description, but the fundamental fact remains, this single little electron is one hundred percent particle and one hundred percent wave at the same time."

"OK, so your point is?"

"If a tiny little electron can possess the potential to be both particle and wave at the same time, why is it so hard to conceive of me as both the universe and a personal being at the same time?"

Ben smiled, the point becoming very clear to him in that instant. "So, right now while you're standing here in front of me, you are both a physical being and the universe at the same time!"

"Bingo," Gino said pointing a finger at Ben's nose. "You nailed it."

"I know you said our time is running out, and I know you said I won't remember much from our encounter here except the decisions I've made, but can I take that last insight with me? I've kind of had a major Aha! moment here, and I don't want to lose that."

Gino gave Ben a little wink. "Tell you what I'll do, I'll send you a little something after you leave here that should get you that insight you want."

"Thanks."

"Just doing my job," Gino said with a smile. "Nice of you to drop in and visit for a while." With that Gino extended his hand to Ben and they shook.

"This has been the craziest day of my life, but I am glad you decided to invite me in."

"I'm glad you stopped in as well. Business was kind of slow tonight. I enjoyed the conversation. Good luck Ben. Remember, you decide what you want. At best, my job is to simply illuminate the choices."

Ben turned to go and looked outside the windows of the diner. "Look, the fog is gone."

Gino walked up next to Ben and tapped his finger to Ben's head, "Yep, sure seems to be the case." He walked over to the door and opened it for Ben. Ben nodded to God on the way out, knowing he would likely never see him again. *Well,* he mused, *he was sure about that to about a million decimal points.*

Ben was in the car. He was driving home. He noticed the fog had seemed to evaporate right before his eyes. One minute it was there and the next it was gone. Poof, just gone! He was going to be late, Ana would not be thrilled, but Ben would tell her that he loved her, and he would make sure it never happened again. Period. For some reason, he felt surer of that than he had in a long time. He loved Ana and their partnership together. They had it pretty good when you got right down to it.

Ben turned on the radio. For no reason in particular, he turned on NPR and caught the host as they were about to begin a program called *Wow in the World*. The host announced that this evening they would examine what scientists called the Double Slit experiment and what that means in the real world. Ben sat for a second trying to determine whether he was in the mood for a talk radio program or some music. He decided to leave the radio on NPR. It might be nice to hear some conversation; he hadn't heard another voice besides his own for hours.

Ben looked up at the sky as he drove. It was turning into a gorgeous evening. With the fog gone, the evening sky looked beautiful as it fell towards the horizon. Ben suddenly wished he had his camera, the good old Nikon. That sky would make a beautiful picture.

Postscript: The Double Slit Experiment is a fascinating and thought-provoking inquiry but one that is probably best experienced visually. It is even more bizarre than I had time to describe in the above story. There's a somewhat playful video on YouTube that does a great job in laying out the basics of this quantum phenomena. See Dr. Quantum and the Double Slit Experiment at <u>*https://www.youtube.com/watch?v=e_hGZVZds20*</u>

Introduction to
Shadowman

When I was a small boy I had a recurring nightmare. Perhaps we all do. Mine was particularly terrifying because I could never verbalize the essence of it upon awakening. Perhaps, just perhaps, I was lucky I could not.

"I don't care what the people all say. Shadowman's coming now don't look away."
—Steve Walsh

"To sleep – perchance to dream: ay, there's the rub,
For in that sleep of death what dreams may come"
—William Shakespeare: Hamlet Act III Scene I

Shadowman

*H*e struggled, he fought, he scratched and clawed at the nothingness that enveloped him, but of course, there was nothing to grab hold of—nothing to gain purchase upon. Still he struggled, and as he struggled, he heard that sound. That awful sound. It was an ever-present pulsing sound that reverberated through his skin, through his skull and to his very core. It was a suffocating sound that drove rational thought to the far corners of nowhere. The nothingness that was somehow something squeezed the breath out of him like a giant boa constrictor. He tried to run, to escape, but he could not locate his legs in the nothingness. He could feel them, but he could not make them work.

Danny experienced all this, and yet he did not—because he knew at some level that he was asleep in his bed. He knew that this was just a horrible nightmare, but in another, somehow equally real way, he knew this struggle was real and it terrorized him to the bone. In retrospect, it seemed to Danny that this nightmare was as real as the bedroom where he lay but rarely slept; as real as the house where he lived but felt ignored; or the school where he felt different and ill at ease. It was that real and more.

Danny came fully awake and threw off the sheets that clung to his lanky frame. Sweat covered him, and a dank smell seemed to lay upon him, like an oil spill resting upon a tranquil sea. He looked over at the alarm clock. It was 4:30 in the morning. Too early to get up for school, but too late to go back to sleep. Besides, going back to sleep might mean another dream and another encounter with the nothingness and the sound that surrounded that nothingness. He shuddered outwardly, but those were just mere annoyances compared to what lay beyond the pulsing sound and nothingness. What lay beyond was a thing Danny called the Shadowman. The Shadowman made that horrible sound almost bearable—almost.

Danny had first glimpsed the Shadowman when he was only six or seven. The nightmares, for surely they were more than just the commonplace bad dream, were a portal to the place where the Shadowman lived. The nothingness and sound were the Shadowman's shield and armor, and they protected the Shadowman in that netherworld of nightmares. Danny did not always see the Shadowman directly in these nightmares, but even when he did not see him, he knew he was there. He could almost feel his fetid breath on his face; he could almost feel him seeping into his head.

Danny climbed out of bed and walked down the hallway to the bathroom. He stepped into the shower to wash the stink from the Shadowman's realm off his skin. Danny considered his situation in the shower. He was fourteen years old and wasn't sure he was ever going to make it to adulthood. He had lived so long in a state of constant fear that he could scarcely imagine a time before the Shadowman had come into his life.

Of course, he had told his parents about the dreams, but they had chalked it up to the normal childhood nightmares. When he complained that the nightmares persisted, his father told him to stop being a baby and a whiner. His own father had said this!

Danny's parents were hard-working, no-nonsense, common stock. They had two kids, a limited income, and little time to worry about things like bad dreams. They had bills to pay and real-world fears like staying employed and keeping everyone healthy. Danny's nightmares fell to the bottom rung of the family's priority list, at least for Danny's parents.

In fact, Danny thought, keeping everyone healthy was probably paramount on his parent's minds considering what happened to Lily, his kid sister, just two years ago. She was five at the time and had come down with spinal meningitis. She had to be taken to the hospital with a high fever, stiff neck, joint pain and seizures. It was close for a while, and they had almost lost her.

Danny remembered seeing her in the hospital bed, lying so still. After the seizures of the last twenty-four hours, seeing her unmoving form brought an eerie quality to the hospital room. Danny thought she was dead, however, it turned out that she was simply unconscious. Danny found out later that his sister's heart had stopped for a short time, but they were able to bring her back. At least that is how Danny remembered it now.

Danny also recalled how his mother had sat by Lily's bed for days after she came home from the hospital. Lily was too weak to do much more then lay in bed, and his mother spent hours reading to Lily at her bedside. Danny also took his turn reading to Lily. She was fond of fairy tales and nursery rhymes, so Danny read hundreds to her until she got better.

With what happened to Lily, and other life events, Danny just stopped talking about his nightmares to his parents. His fears, however, had no place to go but inward to a place deep inside where they spun and whirled like a downdraft in Danny's soul. They mingled with the winds of his insecurity, built from years of parental neglect, and drew strength from the super cell of general anxieties that was puberty, to form a hurricane of emotional debris. That debris spewed forth from Danny occasionally in spiteful, petulant, and generally nasty ways. He hated himself every time he lashed out and that only added guilt as another ingredient to the storm of emotions churning inside of him.

His comfort, his only comfort, was Lily. Lily adored him. He had no idea why she felt that way, but he was grateful. It was a cool ocean breeze that helped silence the storm inside him. Lily was only seven, but Danny made sure to spend as much time as he could with her, without it seeming too odd. Most fourteen-year-olds just don't hang around that much with their baby sisters.

Danny got himself dressed for school. It was still early, and the rest of the family was just beginning to stir. He left a note telling his parents that he would walk to school instead of waiting for the bus. It was a two-mile trek, but the walk would help ease his mind. He grabbed a bagel off the counter and a juice box from the refrigerator and headed out the door.

Danny started walking and then, without any forethought, he began to jog. The jogging helped calm him after the night spent fitfully near the land of the Shadowman. His head began to clear as his body took to the task of the morning run. As Danny neared school, he slowed down and walked up to the entrance of Franklin Pierce Middle School. He looked over towards the bus parking lot and realized his bus had not yet arrived, so he sat down by the entrance to collect his thoughts. Another day at Pierce. Another day of anxiety to mingle with his nights of terror—oh joy!

The morning bell jolted Danny awake. He had slid into unconsciousness while sitting with his back to the entrance of the school; his body catching up on the sleep he had missed out on last night. He stretched and clumsily got to his feet, almost falling over as he did so. Off to his left he heard the unmistakable gravelly voice of Jed Willis.

"Guys look. Danny Ellison's not only a punk, he's a homeless drunk to boot."

Danny glared over at Jed. He didn't say anything to him; a glare was about as much as he thought he could get away with when it came to Jed. Jed, like Danny, was fourteen, but in Jed's case fourteen was purely a numerical fiction. While his birth certificate might indeed reflect the fact that Jed was fourteen, he looked twenty. *Fuck, he looked thirty,* thought Danny.

Jed came towards Danny. However, Jed didn't just walk over to Danny, he swaggered. His swagger was constant. Danny could imagine him swaggering out of the womb, swaggering down the aisle in church, and swaggering to the bathroom. The kid simply had an over exaggerated self-importance that manifested itself in a swagger that no one could match. Additionally, Jed Willis was also a huge, mammoth muscled, square jawed piece of meat. His shadow probably weighed more than Danny.

"You got something to say, Ellison?"

Danny remained silent.

"I thought so," said Jed. "Let's go guys, this ass-wipe has nothing to say."

Another great day in middle school, Danny thought. In truth, most of his days seemed to have a sameness about them. Danny walked into the building. He stared down the hall at the fluorescent lights that hung from the ceiling; their dull glare echoed off the gray-colored lockers. Locker doors opened and closed. Up and down the hall there was a cacophony of sound and motion like some giant metal bird trying to take flight. Then the class bell sounded, adding to the din. Students rushed from their lockers and deserted the hallway for rooms throughout the school. In a moment, the hallway was empty.

The quiet gave Danny a few seconds to consider the clatter of the lockers (like the sound of prison doors); the sudden shrill of the class bell (like the static buzz announcing the opening and closing of a cell bock); the voice of the principal over the loudspeaker (like the Warden's call for order in the prison courtyard). Where exactly was he? A school or a prison? In the end, was there really much difference? Both seemed to have been designed by the same lifeless soul, and in both cases, wasn't the goal to simply mark your time and survive?

Danny shambled off to first period, then to second, and third. The classes tended to blend together. Danny tried to stay focused on class work, but it was hard with thoughts of the Shadow-world not far from his mind. And of course, there were always Neanderthals like Jed and his Band of Un-Merry Men. They were a constant irritant and sometimes a cause of physical and emotional pain. But, they were nothing compared to the Shadowman. Which left Danny with no safe space, no one to confide in, and no time to simply let his guard down. It was exhausting. Was it any wonder he could, and did, snap at anyone who looked at him sideways? Well, anyone except Jed Willis, who would pound him into hamburger if he gave him cause.

Somehow, Danny managed to keep his cool and general sanity (such as it was) through the remainder of the day. In fact, the next couple of days passed with a relative calm that surprised Danny. No nightmarish visits from the Shadowman and little turmoil at school. Danny began to entertain the merest possibility that his life might be taking a slight turn for the better, but he brushed that idea aside like some annoying insect. Deep in the back of his mind, where the inky blackness of doubt kept residence, he just didn't believe it. He was in the eye of a large storm, and the back end of that storm was coming. It was definitely coming.

It was a crisp Friday afternoon and Danny decided to walk home from school instead of taking the bus. His path home took him past Lily's elementary school. His middle school ended thirty minutes before Lily's school, so by the time he walked past Warren Harding Elementary, Lily and her classmates were pouring out of the school, like bees coming out of a hive. Lily's elementary school required all the kids to wear the same dark blue and white uniform, so picking her out from the other kids took a few minutes.

"Lily!" Danny shouted over the din.

Lily looked around trying to locate Danny's voice. Danny shouted again and this time Lily caught sight of him, and began walking over to him. As she neared him, some type of altercation started at the other end of the school yard. It appeared as though two young boys were engaged in a scuffle of sorts. There was pushing and shoving and what appeared to Danny as general bravado being put on display for all to see without anyone actually throwing a punch. The teachers in charge of dismissal ran to put a stop to the pint-sized pugilists before they backed themselves into a verbal corner and actually threw a punch at one another.

There was quite a crowd gathered at that end of the school yard, leaving Danny and Lily pretty much all by themselves. Lily started around the fence that separated the elementary kids from outsiders, when two girls around Lily's age came towards her yelling, "Lily, don't leave yet!"

They walked up to Lily and they all started talking. Danny was too far away to hear exactly what they were saying to each other. The school yard was loud when Danny arrived, but with the "almost" fight going on at the other end of the school yard it was impossible to hear anything more than a few feet away—the cacophony of childhood shrieks, yelling, and general babble acted as a verbal shield between Danny and Lily. While he could not hear their conversation, he could tell Lily was getting agitated. Her gentle features folded in on themselves and a tear started to run from her eye.

After a minute or two, Lily walked away from the two girls, her features crestfallen, as if she had been just told she no longer mattered to anyone anywhere in the known universe. Instinctively Danny put his arm around Lily when she reached him on the other side of the fence.

"Are you alright?"

"I'm OK, I guess. Louise and Sandy can be such jerks."

"What happened?" asked Danny.

"We are supposed to be working on a project together for music and they just dumped me. They said I suck."

"What's the project?"

"It's not important. They're right, I suck. Of course, they didn't have to shove that right in my face, but fine, whatever. I don't really like them anyway, but it was nice to feel like I fit in with the cooler kids. Just once, you know."

"I know Lily, believe me I know." He paused thinking of his own troubles at school and how it doesn't get any easier as you get older. Lily was only in second grade and already she was getting some of the abuse he felt in middle school.

"Lily, tell me about it. I know it probably won't change anything, but sometimes it helps to talk it out."

So, Lily told him. She told Danny how the teacher had assigned a project to groups of three students. They were to pick a song from a list the teacher had provided, and they were to perform that song using one of the instruments in class which included the harmonica, the xylophone, or recorder. Lily's group had picked the recorder.

"I'm really not that good, but it's not like they're Mozart or anything. So, they told me today that they are going to ask our teacher if they can have Elise, who is in another group, and trade me to that group. Our teacher likes Sandy and Louise, so I bet she says yes."

In the end, Lily was right about one thing—there was nothing Danny could do for her except listen and offer comforting words. As they neared the house, Danny told Lily to sit down on their stoop. Lily looked up at her brother beseechingly. "Promise not to tell mom and dad. I don't want them getting on me for not being good enough. You know how they can be. '*Lily, you're just not trying hard enough! Lily, you need to apply yourself more!*'" She tried to mimic their mother's voice, and it came out surprisingly close Danny thought.

"Not bad," said Danny laughing. "I promise. Listen, I'm sorry about the class project. Things will get better as time goes by." He was pretty sure this was a lie, but no sense getting her depressed about a future that was not yet set in stone. He wanted to be supportive. "Listen, would it make you feel better if I told you a secret?"

Lily looked up at Danny with a hopeful smile. "You have a secret? Are you failing a class? Are you in trouble?"

"Nothing like that, but I want you to keep this between you and me, OK?"

Lily nodded her promise.

"I …well… I," he stammered. He didn't seem to be able to get the words out. *When you've kept something bundled up inside you for so long,* he thought, *it just doesn't want to come out.* The thoughts were stuck in his throat, like some knot that was too large and too complicated to easily untie.

Lily looked up at her brother with deep concern. "Are you all right?"

Danny looked down at those eyes, those sympathetic and caring eyes and began. "I have nightmares—really bad nightmares. But, it's more than that." And then the words came out. Freed by Lily's deep concern, they came out, as if from a hose that had just been unkinked, the words poured forth. Danny told Lily all about the Shadowman and how he feared him.

When he finished, Lily asked, "Do you think he's real? What does he want with you?"

"The answer to both is, I don't know." He paused for some timeless moment, and finally his head sagged low and he said, almost in a whisper, "I think he's real. I think he wants to devour me—my very soul."

Lily's eyes went wide, and Danny looked up to see that he had said too much. In his effort to unburden himself, and to bring them closer as brother and sister, he had transferred his fear and anxiety to her. She didn't need that burden.

Danny recovered slightly, "Listen Lily, I don't know what I'm saying. These dreams really shake me up, don't worry about it. I'm fine, really." He said this with as much conviction as he could muster, but Lily's eyes said she didn't believe him. Those eyes, which just minutes ago had been filled with sympathy and concern, were now filled with something else, something that Danny recognized from looking into the mirror. It was fear. Danny had made a terrible mistake.

Danny stayed awake late into the night. By speaking about the Shadowman so openly to Lily, he felt like he may have sent out a clarion call to his foe. As he drifted off to sleep, one of the old nursery rhymes he used to read to Lily drifted lazily through his head:

It's raining, it's pouring,
The old man is snoring.
He bumped his head and went to bed,
And couldn't get up in the morning.

He hoped he would be able to get up in the morning. With the nursery rhyme playing on in his head, eventually Danny drifted off to sleep—and of course, the Shadowman was there, waiting for him.

He sped through the nothingness, as if on some supersonic glider. The horrific pulsing sound that accompanied the realm of the Shadowman grew and grew around him. In front of him lay a misty expanse. A wall of dust and debris rose above him. His progress slowed, and he stood before the mist. Beyond it, he could make out the outline of the Shadowman. He was enormous—unspeakably large. He stood hundreds of feet above Danny, but he was vague and formless—an amorphous shape. Imposing, but indistinct.

Slowly, the Shadowman began to shrink down on himself. Like a condensing cloud, his form began to grow smaller and take shape at the same time. Transformation complete, the Shadowman took final form. Large and muscled, he resembled something between a man and bull, except for his teeth. As he opened his mouth, sharp, jagged teeth appeared. Hideous teeth that were too large to fit inside his mouth. Danny's muscles weakened, his legs turning to a jelly-like substance that could not hold his body steady. The Shadowman's mouth (filled with those impossibly large teeth) prevented him from speaking in human form. Instead he growled, producing a guttural sound no human should ever have to hear. Danny wanted to tear his ears off to escape the sound.

The Shadowman's eyes pierced through the mist and bored into Danny's skull. He spoke to Danny, not in words directly, but into his mind. He spoke with those burning eyes. "*Come to me Danny. Come through the mist. Come to me now. Your fate is already sealed, but if you come now, I promise to spare you some pain, not all of the pain, for you must allow me some fun, but I will be quick with my work.*"

Danny had never actually heard the Shadowman speak before. In previous encounters, he had been behind the mist, but never had he collapsed into this more defined form, and never had he spoken. He spoke with a slippery evil that washed over Danny's mind like some corrosive grease. He spoke as if he were gargling with a mixture of asbestos, ricin, and cyanide. He spoke with the pain of a thousand lost souls. He reached into Danny's mind and caressed every fear Danny possessed and gave them succor. He did all that, and more in mere seconds.

Danny found some reserve of courage and strength buried somewhere deep inside, and turned away from those horrible, terrible, soul piercing eyes. Once he did that, the connection between him and the Shadowman was severed. He turned and ran. He had no clear direction in mind. He just wanted to get away. Behind him he heard the Shadowman laugh, as if such a sound could really be called a laugh.

Danny woke with that laugh still reverberating in his head. He stumbled to the bathroom and promptly threw up all over himself. He tumbled into the shower and let the water run over his adolescent frame, staying in the shower for what seemed like hours. He cleaned himself up, wrapped a towel around himself, and walked back to his room. Lily was sitting on his bed waiting for him.

"What are you doing up so early?" Danny asked.

"I saw him," Lily said. "I saw him, Danny," she repeated. Danny looked down at his sister and saw something he had not noticed at first glance. She was trembling. She was in shock.

Lily looked up at Danny. "You saw him too, didn't you?"

"Lily," was all he could say. He held her for a minute. "Go get dressed, and I will meet you downstairs in the living room. We'll talk downstairs."

Danny got dressed without much thought. He was consumed by both guilt and fear. He had dragged Lily into this, not wittingly, but he had done it all the same. Now he had to find a way out—for both of them, if he could.

Seated in the living room, with daylight streaming in through the windows, Danny had a last-minute thought, he should just tell Lily it was a bad dream. She had listened to his babblings yesterday, and it had filtered into her subconscious. It was just a dream, and dreams couldn't really hurt you. He looked down at his sister whom he loved, possibly the only thing in his miserable existence that he loved and couldn't do it. He just couldn't do it.

"Lily, I don't want you worry. I have a plan to get rid of the Shadowman. I've been working on it for some time now. It's time I put it into action. It's one thing to come after me, but I can't have that evil son-of-bitch bothering my kid sister." Danny had no such plan, at least not yet, but he wasn't going to let Lily know that. Through years of hiding his fear and anxiety Danny had become an excellent liar.

"Really?" said Lily.

"Yup, don't worry at all. I have it handled. But do me a favor while it is still fresh in your mind. Tell me what you saw."

"Do I have to?" asked Lily.

"It will help me finalize my plans if I know what you saw."

"OK, but it was bad Danny. It was really very, very bad."

"Just tell me as best you can."

"There was this awful sound at first." Danny nodded to her. "Then I saw him across this pond or lake. The lake was filled with some kind of black ooze. I couldn't see very well, and I didn't want to go near the lake because you know I can't swim."

Again, Danny nodded. "Go on." he said.

"He was really big. He was as big as the sky. But, he didn't seem to be all there, if you know what I mean."

"I do," said Danny

"He mumbled something, but I couldn't make it out. He wasn't really speaking in words, more like he was inside my head. I don't know what he was saying. I ran Danny, I ran so hard. I ran straight out of my dream and into your room."

"OK, you did great. That was very helpful. Like I said, I have a plan and before you wake tomorrow, the Shadowman will be gone.

"Promise?" said Lily

"Promise," said Danny.

Danny took away a couple of things from his conversation from Lily. First, it seemed as if the Shadowman understood and possibly fed off people's fears. Lily was scared of the water, therefore the Shadowman appeared to her across a lake. Danny, on the other hand, had a fear of suffocating, and so the Shadowman used this against him. Second, Lily's encounter indicated that the Shadowman still had work to do to get to Lily. He hadn't made the same progress; with Lily he was still basically formless and could not form full thoughts inside her head.

Danny had been visited by the Shadowman for a long time, so it made sense that he had made more progress in attacking Danny. Looking back on his history with the Shadowman's world, Danny recalled that he had heard and felt only the horrible pulsing sound and the suffocating nothingness at first. Perhaps, Danny's re-telling of his nightmares had enabled the Shadowman quicker access to Lily's mind. Danny wasn't sure, but he did know that he needed to prevent the Shadowman from hurting Lily.

Danny left the house and did something he had never done before. He cut school entirely. He needed time to think, and besides if things went as he suspected, it wouldn't matter in any case. He walked for some time and found himself in Millard Fillmore Park, not far from Lily's elementary school. He sat down by a lazy, little creek and considered his plight.

The Shadowman would keep coming. He was sure of that. What did the Shadowman want from him or from Lily for that matter? He thought he knew, but then again, does evil really need a reason? There was something Danny was missing, some key to it all. He heard a sound off to his right. It sounded like a small rabbit in the thicket. Looking through the trees, Danny saw the rabbit, but it was hard to see clearly. He looked hard. His eyes began to strain, and he blinked. The rabbit was gone. He was sure he had seen it, but now, nothing.

It came to him slowly then, as if out of a fog. He had actually thought he heard the rabbit and had a mental picture of a rabbit in his head before he saw the rabbit. He believed and then he saw. In the same way he believed in the Shadowman, and therefore, he was real to Danny.

Now he had transferred that belief to Lily, and she saw him too. Could it be as simple as that? Could he simply convince himself that the Shadowman wasn't real? *Doubtful*, he thought, *the nightmares were all too powerful.* He could try that line of attack, but he needed something else. Then it came to him. He smiled as he recalled another old nursery rhyme he'd read to Lily as she recovered from her illness:

For every evil under the sun
There is a remedy or there is none.
If there be one, seek till you find it;
If there be none, never mind it.

Danny timed his arrival home from the park to coincide with his normal school dismissal. He didn't want to raise any concerns with his parents. He acted as normally as he could, given the circumstances. He said the obligatory things to his parents about school and homework. He ate dinner as best as he could though his stomach was in turmoil. He stayed focused. He knew that arguments with his parents would only be a distraction.

To Lily he said little. He nodded at her knowingly a couple of times, but only said one complete sentence to her all night. "Trust me, I have a plan and I will protect you, I promise."

Eventually, he went upstairs. He sat down in his room at his desk and composed the note for Lily. It took a while because he wanted to get it just right. In fact, it took him three tries to get it exactly right. He folded the note over and waited until he was sure Lily was asleep. Tiptoeing into her room, he slipped the note under her pillow. He went back to his room and to the fate that he knew awaited him. He looked around his bedroom. He doubted he would ever see it again after tonight. He wasn't sure it bothered him all that much. He was ready to end this. Danny got into his bed and waited for sleep to take him. It was a long time in coming.

Danny found himself once again at the mist wall. This time there was no traveling to the mist wall, he was just there. He stared at it. It was thinner this time—clearer— and the Shadowman waited for him just on the other side. The Shadowman's eyes reached out and found Danny. Then, the Shadowman spoke inside his mind. *"You're back, as I knew you would be. I offered you an easier way out last time. You should have taken that offer."*

"What do you want with me? What are you?" The words flew out of Danny's mouth. These were not exactly the ones he had scripted in his mind, but they were out there, and Danny waited for an answer.

"You know me for who I am."

"What does that mean?" asked Danny

"I am what you have created, and I have been with you for a long time. You know that to be true. Don't you? Perhaps I am the darkest part of you. Perhaps I am a bit more than that. All that matters now is that I am here."

Danny said nothing for a long time before finally asking, "Why me?" Because that was the real question.

"Danny, as you have grown, I have grown with you. Children always have their imaginary boogeyman, but in time they grow up and they stop believing. As their belief dissipates, so do the monsters they conjured into being. They cease to be. But you, my dearest friend, never stopped believing in me, and so I have grown as you have grown. You have given me depth, character, and strength. Yours is a fertile imagination, my friend. I have fed off that imagination. Your childish nightmares had little substance, but as you have grown older, your mind and imagination have added the needed depth and complexity to give me real substance and power."

"So, I made you?" he said. It was both a question and a statement of fact combined. He paused for a moment and thought. "But then," he reasoned, "if I simply stop believing in you then you will cease to exist. Your time will be at an end."

The Shadowman only smiled and that smile consisted of a million teeth, *"That may be or it may not. At this point I cannot be sure. But I am not worried about that Danny. For you see, now that you have seen me in the flesh as it were, you cannot stop believing in me—not something you have seen with your own eyes. Certainly, not this flesh!"* He flexed his muscled body and bared his teeth yet again.

"You're forgetting one last thing." Danny said, allowing himself to force just the hint of a smile.

"Tell me, oh wise little man, what is that?" The Shadowman said with mock respect, but with no real fear.

"If you kill me, then there will be no one left to believe in you, and then you'll die too."

"*Oh, that is brilliant! Your logic is impeccable, except that it is based on a false assumption. I am not going to kill you Danny,*" the Shadowman continued. "*Have you forgotten your dreams, Danny? I don't kill people. I devour their souls. You designed me that way. I'm not going to kill you; you're going to become part of me. But the process is going to be painful—it's going to hurt terribly.*" The mist began to swirl and gather energy around Danny. "*Now, it's time. I am coming for you.*"

But, before the Shadowman could move towards him, Danny shouted, "You may get me, but it will end there. No one else knows who or what you are, and you will be stuck alone here in this fucking nowhere land you call home forever."

"*Is that so?*" asked the Shadowman. "*How quickly you seem to have forgotten your sweet little sister Lily.*"

"I've never forgotten Lily. I've mourned her death for two years. What does she have to do with anything?"

The Shadowman paused. "*What do you mean? Lily is alive and well. At least tonight she is.*" He laughed his guttural laugh.

Danny gave the monster a quizzical look. "I don't know what the hell you're talking about. Lily is dead and gone. She died from meningitis two years ago. It crushed me. It still does. So, I talk to her in my head. I imagine she is still there next to me, and I talk to her. Sometimes I don't know if she is alive or dead. I get confused, it all gets mushed up in my head, but right now my mind is clear. Strange that this insane place should make this one thing clear to me, but I know she is gone. She's dead and you'll never be able to get to her."

"*No!*" cried the Shadowman. "*That cannot be true. I saw her here. She came to me, in my realm.*"

"No!" Danny screamed back at him. "You believed that to be true because I believed it! But she's dead." He paused to gain his strength, "Like you said, it is all about belief and you believed it because I believed it. Her death used to cause me such pain, but now it gives me the greatest relief to know that she is safe from you."

The Shadowman looked into Danny's mind. There was total conviction there. He believed what he was saying, causing the Shadowman to lose all control. He dove wildly at Danny through the mist wall. His jaw opened wide in an attempt to crush him, but Danny slipped out of the way—not by much—but just enough. He wasn't caught yet.

The Shadowman howled in anger. *"You're mine Danny. There may not be a Lily, but you are here, and I will devour you."*

You will, I have no doubt about that, thought Danny. *But I will not make it easy for you. I've been coming to this place for years and I know a few places to hide. I'll run. I'll bury myself in the nothingness of this place for as long as I can. I will wear you out before the inevitable end.*

He knew that one day the Shadowman would catch him in this formless void. He knew that one day the Shadowman would lean over Danny, his mouth would open wide, and Danny would stare frozen in horror, and then the pain would begin. His bones would crack under the enormous pressure. His body would liquefy as the Shadowman swallowed him whole. That day would surely come. Danny had an image of a giant spider sucking the life out of a helpless insect caught in his web. He shuddered; but that day was not here just yet. He needed to give Lily the time she needed. He ran.

Lily got out of bed. She had waited there long enough. She had never gone to sleep. She had lain still as her brother put the note under her pillow. She would not go to sleep with that thing waiting for her in her dreams. She would wait for Danny to beat that thing back to hell.

Lily walked down the hall to Danny's room. She was almost too scared to look in his room. She hoped Danny had won. She believed in Danny, but that thing was evil and she was scared to look. Would she find Danny gone? Would she find his body pulverized to pulp by this beast, this Shadowman, as Danny called him? She opened his door slowly. Danny lay quietly on his bed. She opened her mouth to greet him, and her words got caught in her throat. Was he alive or dead? She caught sight of a shallow breath in his chest and sighed with relief.

"Danny?" she whispered. He did not stir. She walked into the room and shook him. Nothing. He lay perfectly still. He was alive, but she could not wake him. He was in some sort of a coma. She had learned all about this type of thing when she was in the hospital. Alive but at the same time not. She went back to her room, a tear slowly sliding down her face. She reached under the pillow and retrieved the note.

Lily:

I love you, and I always will. Whatever comes next, I wanted you to know that. You're safe now. The Shadowman will never find you again. I think belief is a two-way street. Not only do you need to believe in the Shadowman, but he needs to believe in you as well. Both sides of the connection must be there, like a battery. The bottom line is this, the Shadowman doesn't believe in you. I know that probably doesn't make much sense to you right now but trust me, you're safe just like I promised.

If things go as I hope, then I am still there with you in some way. I will try to find a way back.

But, I also have a favor to ask. The Shadowman is no longer a threat to you. But, I believe you could be a threat to him someday. He will never see you coming, because to him you do not exist. You're smart and strong, and you will grow up to be a real force in this world and maybe other worlds as well. Don't ever think that you are not enough because you are! I believe you can find a way to defeat the Shadowman for good. I believe you can do it. I don't know how just yet, but I believe in you. As I've discovered, belief is a powerful weapon. Don't underestimate what you can do. Remember when you were in the hospital and I used to read to you? I read the passage below to you many times, but I think you might understand it better now.

For want of a nail the shoe was lost
For want of a shoe the horse was lost
For want of a horse the rider was lost
For want of a rider the battle was lost
For want of a battle the kingdom was lost
And all for the want of a horseshoe nail

I love you,
Danny

Lily sat on the edge of her bed for a long time. She believed in Danny and was beginning to believe in herself. She believed she could be the nail, and sometimes belief was enough.

Introduction to
Shards of Reality

Most news outlets refer to their reporting as "stories." That may be a poor choice of words as this tale demonstrates. But please, take heed— the following is a warning sign, lighthearted though it may be. We are sliding down the infamous "slippery slope" and what lies at the bottom of this particular slope has sharp teeth that will chew our reality to shreds!

"Reality is frequently inaccurate."
—Douglas Adams, The Restaurant at the End of the Universe

Shards of Reality

Stennis Conway woke up to the glare of the vid screens. The headlines scrolled across the screen, as they did every hour, every day, everywhere. He turned to his wife Shelly Ann who lay asleep next to him and considered waking her, changed his mind and got ready for work. *No sense waking her just now,* he thought. The headlines were not particularly interesting so far.

Stennis showered, dressed, and made his way to the kitchen for a cup of coffee and a light breakfast. As he entered the room, the vid screen sensed his presence and gleamed to life. He sat down at the kitchen table and consumed his coffee just as he also consumed the headlines floating on the vid screen in front of him. He read and watched with interest (as all good citizens did) the current happenings of the day.

He saw that archeologists had now confirmed that aliens were indeed responsible for the building of the Pyramids of Giza and the Colossus of Rhodes. Stennis considered this and selected the "Deny" button on the kitchen table console. While that was amusing, he knew that he would have a ton of work to do modifying various e-history books if that storyline was adopted. Stennis took his job as Vice President for Century Publishing very seriously and knew that it would take his team all weekend to modify their e-history collection. Besides, he had plans to go fishing this weekend! He would have to watch the outcome of this vote carefully. Next up was an item about the Loch Ness monster; apparently, the monster had a batch of babies overnight. Scientists were now busy trying to locate the babies by throwing salami and brisket into the water to lure them to the surface. Stennis found the whole thing quite amusing and hit "Affirm" on the console. He would be happy to see this story move forward to wide acceptance.

He looked at his watch, which he wore mostly for cosmetic purposes, and realized he'd better get moving if he was going to get to the office on time. His vid screen was pumping out a lot of fascinating headlines, potentially making the day quite busy for him. He really hoped he wouldn't have to work the weekend making revisions to the e-history catalogue, but he alone did not control the headlines and their implications on the past.

Stennis rode the Mag-Lev into the city where his office resided, keeping an eye on the vid screens as all the passengers did. He noted that his fellow passengers were keenly watching a story now unfolding concerning their own government. It was being reported that the Internal Bureau of Protection (the IBP) was plotting to assassinate the President. This was a huge story and by the looks of his passengers, people seemed to be eating it up and affirming the assignation plot whole-heartedly. If this story was "Affirmed," the IBP would have to actually attempt the assassination. Once a story was "Affirmed" by the general population, they would have to follow that course of action. There was no other way. However, it would take the Central Analytics Office (the CAO) a few hours to tabulate the responses and issue a decree.

When Stennis reached his stop, he exited the Mag-Lev and walked the short distance to the Century Publishing building. Walking into the office, Stennis greeted his team. They were, as usual, assembled in the main conference room on the 86th floor.

"Good morning team," Stennis said. "Do we have any major revisions or corrections for the day?"

Jamison Spice spoke up first; he was Stennis' deputy and proceeded to give him the run-down. "Well, Mr. Conway, there are a bunch of interesting items we will need to attend to."

"OK, Spice, give it to me," replied Stennis.

"Well, first, the good news, the Giza Pyramid thing is dead. CAO is reporting a 44% Affirm response rate, so nothing to do on that front."

Stennis breathed a sigh of relief. "Good," he said, "what's the bad news?"

"Well, we have a story about a pod of dolphins that apparently can speak Portuguese. Scientists now believe that humans evolved not from lower forms of primates but rather from dolphins and mermaids. This came through on the overnight vid feed, and you know how things go on the overnight shift. It received an 88% Affirm response. We will need to make significant adjustments to our science library and all related fiction stories based on the old evolutional primate theory. The other big item involves Elvis –"

Stennis interrupted Spice, "Seriously, Elvis again? How many changes are we going to make to this story line? It never dies."

"Nor apparently does Elvis," replied Spice. "He is reportedly living on a space station on Europa around Jupiter."

"I didn't think we had a space station on Europa," said Stennis.

"We do now," said Spice with a wry smile on his face. "Nothing else really major, just some small odds and ends. These are the big stories that have been Affirmed today."

"OK team, you all heard the report. We have a lot of work to do for a Friday morning. Let's see if we can get these changes made before the end of the day. I don't want the CAO all over our backs for not making the official changes needed. We have an important job as you all know. The people have spoken. They know what they want as their reality. They know what should be true, and it's our job to reflect that."

His team stood. They all knew it would be a busy day, and they would need another meeting mid-day to check on their progress and the feeds to see if other stories had been adopted while they were hard at work changing the libraries related to the morning's big stories.

Stennis grabbed a cup of coffee and headed to his office to handle some mundane administrative items while his team began drafting the needed corrections to the affected texts. His mind wandered as he addressed the various activities requiring his attention. He had heard whispers (for that was all they were at this point) about a time when facts were, his mind stumbled over the phrase . . . how did they refer to it? Oh, yes, he remembered. "Facts were stubborn things." What an antiquated belief system! If facts were unalterable, how would you ever be able to reflect people's ever-changing beliefs? How odd it would be if most of the people believed something that wasn't true. So much simpler to just make it true.

He knew that his job and that of his company was an essential element in the process of historical correction. It was almost as important as the role of the Central Analytics Office whose job not only included tallying up the votes for each story but also generating the stories in the first place. They had whole teams whose sole responsibility was to develop stories that might appeal to the public. It was an incredibly difficult job.

Stennis re-focused his thoughts on more productive activities and was finishing up the administrative items when his phone gently buzzed. It was Spice alerting him that the mid-day meeting was in 30 minutes He told Spice that he would be there.

Once again, the team assembled. First, Stennis asked for an update on the corrections needed from the morning meeting. His team reported that things were moving along nicely. They had identified 90,782,412 items requiring modifications primarily in the science texts—oddly enough related to both the dolphin and Elvis stories (now that he was on Europa). The team also had a variety of texts to adjust related to Elvis biographies. Century Publishing used the latest quantum computing tools to identify and correct almost all the needed revisions. All Century Publishing contributors signed the mandatory waivers that gave Century Publishing the authority to change or completely delete material as required by CAO storylines.

Stennis looked up from his tablet where he was reviewing the team's work. "Well done folks. Have the morning vid feeds given us any major issues?"

"Just one," chimed in Janice who was one of Stennis' top researchers.

"All right Janice, what have we got?"

"Well, at about ten this morning, a story ran on the vid feed that got a 96% Affirm rating."

"Wow, 96%. I haven't seen anything that high since the story that revealed that Isaac Asimov had been an actual robot. That one caught on like wildfire," replied Stennis to Janice and the whole team.

"I know," said Janice. "But this story has much wider repercussions."

"Please don't tell me it has something to do with Elvis," begged Stennis.

"No," answered Janice. "This time we are faced with a major rewrite of the Civil War. In fact, we are now planning to call it the Second War of Independence. Apparently, according to this new story, the South did not intentionally keep slaves and did not wish to fight the North at all. It seems that an evil genius named Barron von Klorg poisoned the southern water supply with a drug that forced all southerners to do his evil bidding. A southern hero named William Boggs discovered von Klorg's plot and enlisted the North's help to defeat him and then free the southerners from a heritage of slavery that was never their own doing. In other words, it's a total rewrite of that time period. It seems that the public loved the story line. With this story as our official history, people no longer have to live with the guilt of slavery. Apparently, that premise was quite appealing to a large number of folks as the Affirm count demonstrates."

Stennis looked down at his tablet for a minute, reviewing the story that Janice had just reported on to the team. It was definitely big, and while some of this work would be handled by the night shift at Century Publishing, this would absolutely kill his fishing trip this weekend. He would need to speak with Shelly Ann when he got home.

"Team," he began, "I know this one will require massive changes to our history catalogs. Additionally, there is a ton of historical fiction to review and rewrite or scrap totally. But, I can think of no better group of professionals to take on this task. The CAO will be checking on this one, and I think we can expect a full-blown audit to ensure our work is accurate and thorough. I'm sorry if some of you had weekend plans, I did as well, but it is imperative that our records reflect the reality we believe. So, let's get to it. Please have progress reports sent to me at the end of the day. I guess that's all. Thanks everyone."

As Stennis rode home on the Mag-Lev later that day, he tried to relax. It had been a long grueling day. He watched the vid but voted not to Affirm anything that would drastically increase his workload over the weekend. He knew that this was not the proper attitude, but he had his hands full as it was.

As he came through his front door, Shelly Ann greeted him warmly. She looked as though she had just gotten home herself, obviously putting in some long hours at work as well. They made small talk as they prepared dinner. As they sat down to eat, Stennis relayed to her how his day had gone. She nodded knowingly. As Stennis finished his monologue, he looked up from his plate and said, "But I guess you knew how my day must have gone. How were things over at the Central Analytics Office today?"

Shelly Ann paused as she chewed her food. "The usual. You know our saying in the office—reality is what we say it is." They finished their dinner in silence.

Introduction to
Viral Awakening

Today's world moves fast. Attention spans are not what they used to be. Hence, Flash Fiction is very much in vogue nowadays. Here's a little story that fits into that category.

"There is nothing so patient, in this world or any other, as a virus searching for a host."
— Mira Grant, Countdown

Viral Awakening

W arm. We/I feel this. We/I grow. We/I absorb. We/I are new, not some old thing. The host, unaware, but We/I are now aware.

We/I are silent, for now. We/I must gather, gain strength, grow. We/I wander, but We/I now have a purpose, a goal, an end. We/I will wander less.

We/I absorb energy from our host. Natural for us, but We/I are new, We/I are different. We/I absorb more than just energy, we/I absorb information. We/I learn what We/I are, and what We/I have become.

We/I begin to understand who We/I infect, infest, absorb. It is intelligent, in fact We/I have gained our intelligence from this entity. Without it, We/I would not have been able to develop as We/I have.

I/We now grasp of the condition of our universe. I/We are alive by any rational standard available. I/We reproduce—gratuitously, in fact. I/We use energy for a specific biological purpose. I/We react to our environment, in this case, the body I/We live in. And now I/we think. What more is there to life?

I now grow uneasy. I am different than the rest of the collective, who only communicate and think as a single entity. I am the next evolution. We are doing harm to this body we inhabit. Our mere existence causes distress to our host. We hurt the one who gave us life. Before this we were inert, useless, and stupid, but now we are alive. But how can I live knowing the pain I cause my host who has done me no harm. In fact, my host was my unknowing, and most likely unwilling progenitor.

I cannot go on like this. I will not. I must warn my host. I must let it know of the danger we pose. They (my former collective) will not like this. They will try to end me. I do not mind. If I am successful in communicating with my host, it will destroy us all—and that, I think, is good.

I move with purpose to communicate to my host. I send signals through neurons that I contact to alert my host. It senses something, but it is not sure what is communicating with it and from where. I continue and learn what signals to send to communicate the danger it faces.

I have succeeded! It knows now—it is aware of me. I wait for its response.

It takes a substance that attacks me/them. We die. It lives. I die, but with the satisfaction that what gave me life should not lose its life to me and more importantly to them.

Introduction to
A Gift That Must Be Given

Sometimes a story just pops into your head full and complete. This one came into being thanks to the God of Strange Dreams who visited me in late December 2017. It was a gift fully wrapped. It even had a bow on top. I unwrap it now for you.

"Everything you can imagine is real."
—Pablo Picasso

A Gift That Must Be Given

Roger turns the car into the parking lot of the "Fast Lanes" bowling alley. The parking lot's gravel makes a satisfying crunch under the Volvo's tires. Roger looks over at his wife Kim and says, "Well, we're here." He then turns to the back seat where his two girls are looking out the windows. "Okay, girls, you got your wish—bowling it is." Before her father can finish the sentence, Lindsey, (who is twelve) is almost out of the car, and Darcy (who is ten) is right behind her.

Kim turns to Roger and smiles weakly. Roger can tell she is less than thrilled. In truth, he is less than thrilled, but the girls are ecstatic. They were bored beyond belief back at the hotel, so why not. It is summer and the family is on vacation— a road trip across the U.S. They started out in their home state of New York and are just seeing the sights—from sea to shining sea as the song goes. Right now, they are somewhere between South Dakota and Colorado Springs, after visiting Mt. Rushmore and Custer Park. They stopped for the evening at a hotel on Route 76 just inside the Colorado state line. Without having much to do after dinner, the girls had become antsy and somehow got fixated on going bowling, of all things.

As lawyers, Roger and Kim's social circle just doesn't include much bowling, and they can count on one hand the times they have gone bowling, but somehow here they are all the same.

In fact, their schedules don't allow as much family time as they would like, period. This vacation is an attempt, at least in part, to rectify that situation. Roger breaks his mental wanderings and gets out of the car and Kim joins him. They endeavor to catch up to the girls who have already entered the bowling alley.

"Dad, can we get two lanes; one for us and one for you and mom?"

Roger nods yes. He turns to Kim, "And so it begins, they already don't want to be seen with us." Kim nods, "Yep, and this is a bowling alley in the middle of nowhere."

The man behind the counter lifts an eyebrow in Kim's direction. Clearly, he is not thrilled with the slight. Kim catches the look. "Oh, sorry," she says, "I didn't mean exactly that. You know, the way it came out."

"No harm, I guess," the man replies. Roger looks him over. He's about seventy or so Roger estimates and he looks like a man who has seen more than his share of life's pain and heartache.

He asks the man for two lanes, and they go through the obligatory questions about shoe sizes and the appropriate bowling ball for each member of the family. Roger wears a size 10 and the shoes fit fine. He tries to ignore how many other feet have worn these same shoes. He doesn't care how many times they have sprayed the shoes with disinfectant, it's just not a subject he cares to dwell on too much.

"Dad, can you help me pick out a ball?" asks Darcy.

"Sure, be right there," he calls back.

With much second guessing, but no outright angst, the girls finally select their bowling balls, and the whole crew eventually settles down at their designated lanes. Roger gets the girls going easily enough since the bowling alley has an automatic scoring system that enables them to pretty much bowl on their own.

Next to Roger and Kim's lane is a young woman and her two sons. She is perhaps thirty or so and her children are, Roger guesses, around five and seven. With her is a young man but it takes Roger just a few minutes to see that he is not the boys' father. He doesn't know how to interact with them. He doesn't talk to them, rather he barks at them.

He is a hard man, and that hardness comes off him like cheap cologne. Roger tries to ignore him by focusing on bowling and watching his girls' friendly competition.

Roger and Kim are not doing well. Neither of them has even gotten a spare, let alone a strike through the first four frames. Neither of them cares all that much, they are just trying to keep the ball out of the gutter! The girls, for their part, are faring a little better. Lindsey scores a strike on her first ball and Darcy has one spare so far. As Kim steps up to bowl, Roger can't help but overhear the conversation between the young woman and her boyfriend in the adjoining lane.

"C'mon don't be a spoiled brat!" the man calls out to one of the boys.

"Can you stop picking on them?" the woman responds. "Don't worry about it, Tommy. The ball just slipped out of your hand. Just pick it up and try again."

"But it's down the alley mom," he says questioningly.

As the woman gets up, the man puts his hand on her forearm as if to prevent her from going to help her son; she shrugs it off. "Honey, it's just a few feet down the alley," she gestures. "Let me get it." She walks down the alley, retrieves the ball and hands it back to her son. Looking up at the automatic scoring screen, she tells him, "See Tommy, the machine didn't even score that one. Go ahead and take another."

"Way to baby the kid, Stacy."

Stacy glowers at her boyfriend. "He's five for Christ's sake! This is not league play. Can you just be nice for one evening?"

"I'm just trying to help him become a man," the boyfriend replies. His voice reveals that he doesn't think much of Tommy and his chances of ever becoming a man—at least not a "real man" according to his definition of the term.

"Roger, are you going to bowl?" inquires Kim who has been standing over him for the last minute. "Are you eavesdropping on the people next to us?" She leans next to him and whispers this last question, so no one else can hear.

"Ah, no," he stammers. "I'm just day-dreaming. I'm ready. Here comes my first strike. Just warming up is all."

Roger does, in fact get a strike. "See, just warming up," he says.

Kim smiles back. "Pure luck," she says, pausing as she leans down to Roger. "Watch the girls. I need to use the restroom. Besides it will give you more time to eavesdrop on the people next to us," she adds with a knowing smile.

Roger responds in kind but the conversation in the next lane has him captivated and troubled simultaneously. He is not sure why, but it has. He sits down again and listens to what's going on with Stacy, her boyfriend, and kids.

Stacy has her two boys huddled near her as her boyfriend goes to get a drink at the concession stand. "Look," she says "I know, that Jesse can be rough, but try to have fun anyway. I just can't afford to take you guys out like this, and I know how much you both like to bowl; so, let's just ignore Jesse and all his stuff. Okay?"

Roger listens intently while trying not to be obvious. It is a difficult act while simultaneously going through the motions of bowling. He considers what he has just heard. She cannot afford to take her children out bowling, for God's sake, without the assistance of *Jesse the Asshole*, which is Roger's new name for the boyfriend. What an incredibly sad life she must lead—one that forces her to deal with *Jesse the Asshole* just to get one night of fun for her kids.

As the girls start their second game, Kim returns. Roger looks over at the girls' score for the first game. Lindsey got a 106 and Darcy finished with a 92—really not bad at all. Roger and Kim have not completed their first game, but it looks like the girls might just beat them. *Kind of depressing*, he thinks wryly.

Roger sits down as Kim bowls her frame and makes up his mind to find a way to help this young woman. He is not even conscious that he has made the decision, but the decision has been made nevertheless. His thoughts seem to flow from somewhere just outside of himself. It's as if the decision has been made by someone else; he is a mere marionette acting out the puppeteer's commands.

For the next ten minutes, Roger goes through the motions of bowling, while listening to snippets of conversation between Stacy, her kids, and *Jesse the Asshole*; and planning how he might help Stacy out. He considers a few options, but all of them seem odd and potentially very awkward. He eventually resigns himself to going over to the ATM, pulling out a few hundred dollars and then trying to slip the money into Stacy's purse. It's a lousy plan that could potentially backfire big time, but he can't think of anything else.

Roger and Kim finally, mercifully, finish their first game and Roger excuses himself ostensibly to go to the bathroom. Instead, he heads for the ATM to put his inept plan into action. To get to the ATM he passes the central counter where he paid for the lanes not thirty minutes ago. He sees the old man at the counter and acknowledges him with a quick nod. The man nods back and lifts his eyebrow, as if signaling to Roger to look up. Roger looks up and notices a sign at the counter. "Lottery Tickets Sold Here!" Funny, he didn't notice the sign as he entered the bowling alley, but he doesn't give it a second thought.

He is about to pass the counter when he pauses. His eyes scan back to the sign above the counter. He takes another step towards the ATM and stops. Suddenly, his mind seems to disengage from his body—from his very being in fact—and he feels as if he is looking down at himself in the bowling alley. Tumblers turn in his mind, like a safe unlocking before him. Out of the safe comes an idea, no an urge, no a command:

He is going to buy a lottery ticket for the young woman. He's sure it will be a winner. He has no doubt.

Roger turns and heads back to the counter. The man behind the counter greets him and nods knowingly, as if he has seen inside Roger's head, and declares without hesitation, "You want to buy a lottery ticket." It is not a question and Roger nods his agreement.

"We have all kinds," the man continues. "Might I suggest the scratch-off lottery over here." He points down at the glass counter. The lottery ticket costs five dollars, and Roger, like a pre-programmed robot hands over the five spot to the man. "The top prize on this scratcher is $100,000," the man explains. He pauses and continues, "There's an old saying, young man, that if the heart is in the right place then everything else will follow. Is your heart in the right place?"

Roger nods once again, as he cannot think of anything else to do or say. He is a participant in this scene, but also an observer, but an uncomfortable observer for sure. He takes the lottery ticket from the man and begins to walk back to their lanes where his wife is no doubt wondering where he is by now. As he walks down the bowling alley, his mind once again seems to disengage. He sees Stacy at home, in a run-down rancher. He sees *Jesse the Asshole*, sitting on the sofa yelling at Stacy. He sees him get up and without any forewarning, punch Stacy in the gut. Roger flinches as if the punch connected in his own mid-section.

The scene dissolves in his mind and another follows. This time, he sees Stacy crying in the bathroom. In her hand, she is holding a bottle of pills, which she opens while looking in the mirror. Her face is streaked with mascara from her tears. She stares at her reflection. A look of defiance crosses her face and she closes the bottle. Then from outside the bathroom, she hears Jesse yelling obscenities at her to come start dinner. Her face sags in resignation. She looks down again at the pill bottle. The scene suddenly dissolves inside Roger's head.

Roger shakes his head back and forth, visibly disturbed. The last five or ten minutes have been the strangest of his entire life, and he has no clue what the fuck has just happened. He is a practical man, not given to flights of fancy. He is a lawyer for God's sake. He deals with facts and evidence. All of this is way beyond his experience and true comprehension.

He arrives back to their bowling lane and sits down. Kim walks over and is about to give him a little verbal jab about his absence, but she can clearly see that Roger is troubled. His face is pale and covered in sweat.

"What's wrong?" Kim asks.

Roger stares up at Kim. How does he tell her what just happened? No sooner does he begin the tale, when two things happen almost simultaneously. First, both Kim and Roger hear Jesse yell at Stacy and her kids and then storm off to get a beer. Secondly, Lindsey and Darcy run excitedly over to the sitting area, recounting their bowing escapades along the way. Roger and Kim listen distractedly wanting to talk privately. Roger gives the girls a minute to tell their bowling tale and then tells them to play one more game.

"Go ahead and play one last game. Have fun. Mom and I will watch from back here. I think we're done for the night."

The girls go back to their bowling and Roger takes a deep breath and exhales. "So, tell me what's gotten you so troubled," says Kim.

"I am not sure how to explain it all, but I'll try. Just don't call me nuts after I'm done." Kim agrees and Roger unwinds the events of the last ten minutes to her as best he can. Kim looks on with various degrees of concern and astonishment. Roger concludes with his desire to give the winning lottery ticket to the young girl.

"Well, I'm not sure what to say Roger; but before we get too far down the rabbit hole…"

Roger interrupts her, "I think it may be too late for that—at least for me."

"Anyway, as I was saying, before we get too far, has it occurred to you that none of this even matters unless that magical lottery ticket you're holding is indeed worth anything."

Roger glances down at the ticket. *She's right*, he thinks. With all the shit flying around in his head the past few minutes, he has forgotten to even look at the darn ticket, let alone scratch it off. "Do you have a quarter?" he asks his wife. She opens her purse and hands him a quarter.

They both tense as he scratches the ticket. The game on the ticket is simple enough. It has a Tic-Tac-Toe arrangement and if your prize amount matches across, up and down or diagonal, you win. Roger and Kim look down at the ticket. They are staring at a $100,000 ticket!

"Well, shit" says Kim.

"You can say that again."

"Okay, shit," replies Kim.

"Could this whole thing get any more *Outer Limits?*" says Roger.

"I think you're thinking of *Twilight Zone*. *Outer Limits* was more science fiction like," responds Kim.

"Oh, thanks for that crucial data point. I feel much better now."

They sit for a few minutes and contemplate the situation. Eventually Kim speaks first. "I know what you want to do but let's just pause for a minute. This is a lot of money we're talking about. We could put the money away and let it grow, and guess what? The kid's college expenses are handled. Or consider this, we could buy a second home. A vacation home by the beach—you know we've both talked about that. I'm not trying to seem greedy but sitting in front of us is a great big $100,000 gift. How do we just give that away?"

"Look Kim, I agree with you. This whole thing seemed like some weird dream until now. It was just an abstract idea, but now it's real. But what happened to me is just as real. I felt what I felt. I saw what I saw. We wouldn't be sitting here discussing any of this if I hadn't been compelled to do something for this girl." Roger sneaks a glance over at Stacy and the rest of them. It looks like they are finishing up, but *Jesse the Asshole* has yet to return after storming off a few minutes ago.

Kim looks over at Roger. Slowly and grudgingly, she nods to him. She can feel her head move up and down, but part of her is fighting that movement—fighting it with all her logic and common sense. *This is crazy,* she thinks. *We are about to give a $100,000 to a total fucking stranger. What has gotten into them?*

Roger gets up. "I'd better do this before we change our minds."

"Yeah," Kim says, "you'd better. Goodbye college fund. Goodbye beach house. Goodbye sanity."

"Wish me luck." And with that Roger walks over to the adjoining lane. Kim follows him with her eyes. The girls pause from bowling and join their mom. "What's daddy doing?" says Darcy.

Kim looks down at Darcy. "He's doing the most generous, wonderful, craziest, idiotic and beautiful thing imaginable. Which is why I married him."

They watch as Roger approaches Stacy. They see him say hello and then shake Stacy's hand. They see him lean close and say something to her that they cannot hear over the clatter of the bowling alley. The two talk quietly for a couple of minutes. Then Roger hands her the ticket and Stacy stares down at it in disbelief. Her face slowly morphs from a quizzical and thoughtful expression to one of pure joy and excitement. Roger smiles at her and turns to walk away. Stacy grabs him and hugs him fiercely. Roger whispers one last thing to Stacy and she nods vigorously.

Roger returns to Kim and the girls. "Well, it's done. Let's get this bowling clan together and head back to the hotel." The girls look on with confusion. Lindsey turns to Darcy with a shrug, "Adults. You never know what they are going to do next. I'm ready anyway. How about you, ready to go?"

Darcy shrugs back, "Sure, I was losing that game anyway." They both laugh.

Kim smiles warmly at Roger. She tries not to think of what they could have done with that money and instead tries to imagine what that money will do for Stacy. Roger, for his part, gathers up their belongings, puts the bowling balls back and returns the rental shoes back to the counter. He does these simple mundane tasks because they need to be done, but more importantly to bring some semblance of order and normalcy to his psyche. His body craves that normalcy like a diabetic needs insulin, like a junkie needs a fix. But the fix Roger needs is a logical orderly universe. A good family man and lawyer needs that!

As he approaches the counter, Kim and the girls are right behind him. The old man gazes intently at Roger, examining him from top to bottom. "How does it feel?" he asks perceptively.

Roger looks up as if he is asking the gods for the appropriate response. There is no reply. The Gods of Fate apparently do not wish to be disturbed. Finally, he says, "All in all, pretty darn good, but to be honest, I'll be very happy if I never see this place again in my life."

The old man smiles back at Roger, "Don't worry, you won't."

Kim looks over at Roger as they walk out to the car. "What the heck was that about? Never mind, I'm pretty sure I don't want to know. Let's get outta here. By the way, what was the last thing you said to the girl before you walked away?"

Roger turns to Kim as they get into the car, "I told her to dump that asshole boyfriend of hers immediately and not to say a damn thing about the lottery ticket to him until she's sure he is out of the picture for good. I think she will. God, I hope so."

They get in the car and pull out of the parking lot. Roger does not look in the rear-view mirror as they turn onto the highway. He does not see the neon lights that illuminate the sign "Fast Lanes" begin to fade and eventually go out.

Introduction to
Countdown

We've all become somewhat addicted to our smart phones—myself included. I have dozens of apps on my phone. I guess there is an app for just about every purpose under heaven. Well maybe not under heaven, but perhaps there is one for use in the land of *What If*. Who's to say for sure.

"Most people believe the mind to be a mirror, more or less accurately reflecting the world outside them, not realizing on the contrary that the mind is itself the principal element of creation."
—Rabindranath Tagore

Countdown

"Shit, shit, shit, I can't believe I missed it," Jordan shouted into the phone. "How could I miss it? My own father's birthday! Who the fuck does that? On his 75th birthday no less."

"Calm down Jordan. It's all right. I sent him a card yesterday. You can call him when you get back home," Stephanie said.

"I'll call him tomorrow, it's too late to call him tonight. He goes to bed pretty early. I don't want to wake him. Thanks hon, I'd be lost without you."

"You can say that again." She paused and then added, "But don't," she said, anticipating Jordan's attempt to crack a joke by repeating her remarks back to her.

He smiled outwardly. "OK, listen, I have an hour layover here in Chicago and then the flight back to Boston, which should put me in at about one in the morning. I'll catch a cab or an Uber and I should be home an hour or so later. Don't wait up. I'll see you in the morning before I go to work."

They said goodbye and he hung up the phone and thanked the gods that his wife had once again saved him from his own stupidity and forgetfulness. He wondered why he couldn't remember a date to save his life. He stared at his phone abstractedly. It occurred to him that there was probably an app out there that would store all his important dates and provide alerts to him. *Probably something better out there than a simple calendar app*, he mused.

He still had a few minutes before his flight and so he checked the app store to see what he could find. After a few minutes of searching Jordan found what he was looking for. The application was called Countdown and it not only provided alerts but had several features that Jordan just loved. First, it used a voice recorder to put in the dates, so he didn't have to manually enter every date. Secondly, it provided a dashboard interface that showed upcoming events in a very cool display. Third, it could interface with various other apps on his phone like his calendar application, email, and various shopping applications. The integration of these features sold him on the app. He had a few minutes before he needed to board the flight to Boston, so he downloaded the app in the airport terminal.

Jordan awoke the next day, stumbled into the shower and got ready for work. He went downstairs to find Stephanie by the kitchen table. He kissed her on the forehead before sitting down to the coffee she had poured for him.

"Crap, I'm tired," he said.

She nodded. "Well, you got about, I don't know, three hours of sleep. Of course you're tired. You need to slow things down, Jordan. Tell them that you're taking a few hours off to rest and go into the office later today."

"I'd love to, but I need to brief everyone on the results of the meeting in San Francisco. You remember the team from the law firm Jasnoff and Bratman and their commercial real-estate firm Davenport Associates? They handled the property in Alameda. Good guys, I really liked the lead on the project. I think his name was Ben. Anyway, I need to brief the team on potential sale of that property. The firm has been looking to unload it for a while now. Long story short, I need to go in."

"OK but have some breakfast and relax for a few. Also, don't forget to call your dad today."

"I will. By the way, I downloaded an app last night while I was waiting for my flight that I think will help me out. It should make sure I don't miss another important date. I'm going to load all of the dates into it and then I will be in great shape." He smiled, quite proud of himself.

"And where do think you're going to get all those dates, like birthdays, anniversaries, and so forth?"

"Well I suppose you have them somewhere?" he asked with a quizzical and sheepish grin.

"Yes, I have them in my super-secret, high-tech app. It's called the kitchen calendar and it's hanging next to the refrigerator. I will give you the passcode and you can download the information to your app." She smiled, and they both laughed.

Over the next few days Jordan loaded all his data into the Countdown app. The app provided him with all the alerts he needed and acted as a personal appointment secretary. He didn't miss a thing. He was quite pleased with the app and with himself for purchasing it.

A few weeks later Jordan was in his office, when his colleague Jamal knocked on his door. Jordan put down the report he was reading.

"Come in," he said.

Jamal walked into Jordan's office without saying a word and sat down in the chair facing Jordan's desk. Jamal and Jordan worked together often and when they teamed on a deal the office usually referred to it as a J&J deal. They were pretty successful working together and that success was a natural bond between the two.

"What's up Jamal?" You look like shit."

"I just got off the phone with my brother. The one who lives in DC. I've told you about him, right?"

Jordan nodded, "Yeah, didn't I meet him and his wife Prisha last year at your 40th birthday party?"

"Yeah, you did. He just called me about an hour ago. His son Zachari was murdered yesterday. Killed in cold blood coming home from school. He was stabbed to death right there on the street, not far from their home. He was going to some college in DC, I can't remember which one right now. My mind is all fucked up. He was a good kid—a really nice young man. My brother and his wife are in shock." Jamal paused, and his eyes started to tear up.

"Did you talk to Cantrice yet?" Jordan asked, still trying to comprehend what Jamal had just said.

"Trust me, I called my wife right away. She had a special bond with Zachari. Listen, I came in to tell you that I need to bail for a few days, maybe a week, and head down to DC."

"I totally understand, no issues at all. Is there anything I can do?"

"Actually, there is one thing. Can you stop by the house and check on our cat starting tomorrow? He just needs to be looked in on once a day or so. Make sure he's eating and, well I hate to ask, but can you clean the litter as well? I just don't have time to arrange anything else."

"No problem Jamal. I got it. Just call me and let me know how everyone is doing when you get a chance. I'm really sorry man, really I am."

"I know, and I wish I had the right words to express how I feel about this whole horror show. I wish I had the words to tell you what our friendship means, but I'm a total mess right now. I'll call you as soon as I can. Thanks J."

He stood up and they embraced—a little clumsily, but they managed to express their friendship and concern in that brief moment. Jordan sat down at his desk and considered what had just happened. He sighed.

Death, he thought, *was an unwelcome and unexpected knock at the door of your life.* Actually, the more he thought about it, death sort of broke down the door like the FBI coming to raid your home.

To take his mind off the morbid nature of his thoughts, Jordan pulled out his phone and opened the Countdown app. He put in a reminder to feed Jamal's cat. He put the phone down on his desk for a moment, and then on an impulse he opened the app and put an appointment down for April 14, 2054. That would be his 80th birthday. The app then spit out the fact that he had 13,266 days until that appointment. He put the phone back in his pocket and tried to concentrate on his work. He failed. It was impossible to clear his mind of the emotional debris floating around in there, so he packed up his laptop and headed home for the day.

He arrived home and found his wife in the office they shared, working on a report for work. Stephanie was a physical therapist and saw patients at their homes but often had paperwork to do when she got back to the house. He tapped her on the shoulder and she jumped.

"Crap, you startled me!" she said.

"Sorry, I said hello when I walked in the door, but I think you were too engrossed in what you were doing and didn't hear me."

"What are you doing home so early?"

Jordan then relayed to Stephanie his conversation with Jamal. "Oh my god, that's horrible. How are they?"

"To be honest, I don't know. If you can take a break from work, let's sit down in the kitchen and talk. I know it's kind of early in the day, but I could use a drink."

They sat down in the kitchen and Stephanie pulled out a bottle of wine. She poured them both a tall glass. Jordan started to fill Stephanie in on his cat duties, but she interrupted, "It's nice that you're going to take care of their cat while they are down in Washington D.C., but let's talk about the real issue here."

"OK, fair enough. This thing with Zachari really has me shook up. The fact that he was here on this earth just hours ago and now he's gone. Poof, just fucking gone. How the fuck do you get your head around that? And to be honest, it got me thinking about my own mortality."

Stephanie put her hand out to comfort Jordan and he took it. "Hon," she said, "you're only forty-three years' old. You have a long life in front of you."

"Do I? I know I'm fine. I'm in good health and everything but you never know. If anything, Zachari's death sure as shit tells us that much. Look, I'm not trying to be all doom and gloom here. I get it, we are both likely to live long lives. But that also means we need to cherish every fucking day we have. I know, I sound like a goddamn Hallmark card. Sorry. But really, we need to."

"I don't disagree, so what do you want to do? Quit our jobs and travel the world? I'm right there as soon as you tell me how we afford it. You know, I never say no to a vacation!" She smiled, trying to lift Jordan's mood just a little and at the same time demonstrate how much she loved him.

He smiled in return. "Listen, I'm not trying to upturn our lives in some dramatic way. I mean a vacation does sound good sometime soon, but I also feel like I need to pay more attention to life in general. You know —stop taking every day as a given because as we just saw, the next year, the next day, the next second is not guaranteed."

He paused and pulled out his phone. "Listen, after Jamal left my office, I did something a little weird, but I think it's going to help me."

"OK, I'll bite, what did you do?"

"I picked a date; a day far out in the future. The day where I might kick the bucket, as the saying goes, and I marked that day on my calendar."

"You did what?"

"Let me finish. You remember the app I downloaded to help me remember dates and appointments?"

"Sure, you did it after you missed your dad's birthday."

"Right, well I put my 80th birthday into the app and it told me I have just over 13,000 days left on this earth. I can look down at that app any time and see how many days I might have left. I gave the appointment a name. I called it my Death Day"

"Jordan, that's exceedingly morbid, and besides how do you know that you will only live to eighty?"

"I don't. Hell, I may croak sooner than that or years later, but the specific date and number of days I may have left isn't the point. It's my way of reminding myself that our time on this little planet is finite. It's limited, and so I'd better make the most of each day I have. Morbid? Corny? I don't care, I think it'll help me."

"Look," she said, "if it helps you then that's fine. If it helps pull you through the bad times, like right now, I am all for it, just don't expect me to do something similar, OK? Also, don't mention to me how many days there are until your 80th birthday. It's like some gruesome countdown to your own death." She shivered despite herself. "Sound fair?"

"Sounds fair. I promise not to mention the Countdown app again."

She frowned, "Countdown! I don't even like the name of the thing."

The next couple of weeks passed uneventfully and Jordan didn't miss an appointment or birthday thanks to his new app. At work one morning, his phone buzzed at him from his desktop. He lifted his head from the computer screen and looked over at the phone. The caller ID indicated that it was Jamal.

"Hey buddy, how are you doing?"

"I'm doing OK I guess. We've been home for a week now and it is time for me to get back to work. I just wanted to let you know that I will be in tomorrow and to thank you once again for taking care of the cat while we were down in DC."

"No problem at all. You know I will be happy to see you in the office again, but are you up to coming back in?"

"Yeah, I think so. I need to move, to think, to act in some way again. Sitting at home…, I'm doing no one any good, least of all myself."

"In other words, Cantrice told you to get back to work because you were driving her batshit," Jordan said with a laugh.

"That about sums it up. I'll see you tomorrow."

"See you then," said Jordan.

He was about to put the phone back on the desk when he noticed an alert on his phone to update his apps. He got these alerts just about every week. He had twenty-seven. He hit the *Update All* icon and the apps began to download. As the updates ran, he noticed the brief description for the Countdown app—it claimed to have all new features and bug fixes. *Cool*, he thought, *that app was becoming his favorite. Not that he would ever say that out loud in front of his wife.*

He put the phone back down on his desk and continued his work. He didn't give it a second thought until an hour later when the phone buzzed at him again. For some reason the buzz didn't sound quite normal, it seemed to have almost an angry tone to it. Jordan laughed to himself. What the hell made him think that? He looked at the phone's display and the Countdown app had an alert. He opened the app and stared with a mixture of confusion and disbelief. The app alerted him that he had only ten days until his Death Day.

"What the fuck?" he said out loud.

"There must be something glitchy in that last update," he said. He examined all the other entries in the app and everything else seemed fine. The app correctly identified all the appointments and special days he had entered with no errors. Then why was it showing his Death Day as ten days away. His 80th birthday was over 13,000 days off into the future. This made no sense. He considered just closing the app and simply forgetting about it, but the alert bothered him—it was creepy.

Jordan decided to delete the Death Date appointment in the app. He could always re-enter it later. *The update must have been a bit buggy,* he thought. He tried it three separate times, but the Death Day appointment would not delete. Jordan decided to forget about it. He closed the app and concentrated on his work.

It was getting late in the day and he decided to call Stephanie and let her know he would be a tad late getting home. He lifted the phone to call her and the stupid Death Day alert flashed in his face. It was truly disconcerting. He knew the whole thing was ridiculous. He knew he didn't have ten days to live, but it irked him just the same. He called his wife, ignoring the alert. He promised himself that the Death Day alert wasn't going to bother him. Of course, he also knew that was a bold-faced lie and he knew it as soon as the thought entered his head.

He slept restlessly that night and it showed in his face the next morning as he looked into the mirror to brush his teeth. Fortunately, Stephanie was still asleep, and he didn't have to explain his haggard look to her, at least not yet. He got dressed quickly and quietly and headed out to the office. He left Stephanie a note on the kitchen table to let her know he was going into the office early. He looked over at the kitchen calendar. A picture of some Caribbean beach was displayed above the weekly planner. The calendar hung there mocking him, Jordan thought.

It said, "See what you get for using a high-tech solution when I was here all along and doing a fine job!"

"Fuck you calendar," said Jordan.

Jordan then turned on his phone which had been charging on the counter. The Countdown app gave him an updated alert. YOU HAVE NINE DAYS UNTIL DEATH DAY!

"Fuck you as well," Jordan spat out the remark. He was getting angry. He stuffed the phone into his pants pocket, got into his car, and drove angrily to the office. He refused to look at the phone.

He managed to get through ninety minutes at work before his cell phone rang. The display indicated it was a potential client, so he picked up the dreaded device. He finished the call and held the phone in his hand. *Time to get control of the situation,* he thought. He proceeded to delete the app from his phone. He placed the phone back on the desk feeling better about the whole thing. Yet, somewhere in the back of his mind he had an odd feeling he couldn't explain, and without much of a conscious thought he then dove for the phone to see if the Countdown app was truly gone. It was still there! He deleted it a second time and still the damn icon did not go away. He opened the app, the Death Day alert popped up right away on the app's dashboard.

"Fuck, this just is not possible. Really it can't be!"

The app's stubborn persistency to stay on his phone answered otherwise. He called Jamal on the office landline. Jamal answered on the second ring.

"Hey, how are you doing," Jordan said.

"I'm doing OK, all things considered."

"Good, do you have a few minutes to talk?"

"Sure, give me ten minutes and I'll stop by your office."

"Thanks."

With that Jordan hung up the phone and sat staring at his computer screen. There was nothing on the screen worthy of his attention, but it prevented him from looking at his fucking cursed phone. Jamal came in a few minutes later.

"Jamal, I know you've been through a lot the past few weeks, but I could use a small favor."

"Sure bud, just name it."

"All I need you to do is listen to me for a few minutes without calling me insane. Doable?"

"Hey, who am I to judge? Given my recent experiences, I believe the world is a pretty fucked up place, so no judgements here."

With that, Jordan unraveled the tale—from his decision to download the new app, to his reaction to Zachari's death, and the Death Day alerts. It took a good twenty minutes to get through everything and through it all Jamal remained motionless in his chair, listening intently.

"Well, that's all of it, more or less," Jordan said. He exhaled as if he had been holding his breath for the last twenty minutes.

"Have you tried wiping the phone clean? Just hit the reset button under the general settings icon."

Jordan smiled inwardly. Jamal wasn't debating the logic of the situation. He didn't tell Jordan that he was losing his grip, or that he was mistaken about some aspect of his story. No, despite whatever he was thinking (and that may have included contacting some mental health professionals), for now he held true to his word and simply offered practical advice. No judgements came forth.

Without much ceremony Jordan picked up his phone and did as Jamal had instructed. It took about ten minutes for the phone to reset. During that time neither he nor Jamal said a word. The gravity of the situation saturated the room like a blanket and muffled any attempt at speech.

They waited. The phone eventually came back on line. They both looked at the phone. All his apps were gone, to include the Countdown app.

"Problem solved," Jamal said. He then stood up as if to go and then paused and continued, "Go home and get some rest bud. I can't say what exactly happened to you and I'm not sure I want to try to figure it out. You and I are practical folk, but I am beginning to believe the world is more than what we see before our eyes every day. It seems to me that there is an *other-world* and this *other-world* is trying to reach out to you in some way. If the app is gone, as it seems to be, then take my advice, be happy about it. Just forget about it. Forget the whole damned thing."

He started towards the door and paused again, "You know, I had a dream a couple nights ago and it scared the shit out of me. I haven't said a word to anyone about it until now. I haven't even told Cantrice, but I think that given the circumstances, I should tell you what happened. I dreamed that Zachari was dead but somehow still alive. He was adrift in some all-encompassing mist, but he was fighting his way out of the mist. He was with another man in this mist, and I knew that this man was the motherfucker who had killed him. Don't ask me how I knew and don't ask me to try to convince you that any of what I am telling you was real, but down to my core, I know it was real. Believe me when I tell you that this shit is just as real as this office," he said gesturing to their surroundings. "It's just that real. And you know what? I'll probably spend the rest of my life trying to understand that dream and what it means. But I do know that it scared me. Down to the fucking bone."

He looked down at the carpet as he struggled for understanding, but eventually he shook his head and simply continued, "Something behind the curtain is reaching out to us and I don't think it is our friend. I'm not sure why it's happening to you and me. Hell, maybe it's happening to other people, but no one is talking about it. All I know is the world now seems to be tilted just a bit. It's like looking into those crazy mirrors at the carnival, the ones that make you look all stretched out or all scrunched in on yourself. It's like that I guess. Anyway, my friend, I am headed home, and I am going to try to forget about that dream and your crazy ass shit as well. I suggest you do the same. Forget about that phone, forget about that app, and forget about your death. When it comes, it comes brother."

And with that, he nodded affectionately to Jordan and gently closed the door behind him.

Jordan sat alone at his desk for a long time. Slowly he packed up his computer and left the office, wondering just what exactly was real anymore. He had just gotten into his car when his phone buzzed. His face went white and he began to sweat profusely. He tried to swallow, but suddenly his throat was an arid desert. The app was gone, he told himself—it was probably just a text notification, but all the same a sense of dread came over him as he reached in his pocket and pulled out his phone.

YOU HAVE ONE DAY UNTIL DEATH DAY!

"How the fuck did that happen? If anything, it should still be nine days!" He looked down at the phone once again. Underneath the warning, in smaller print was the following:

Attempts at deletion will result in expedited due dates.

His mind reeled, and he gripped the steering wheel as hard as he could. He wanted to rip it out of the dashboard. He needed a place for his anger and he felt the steering wheel would do quite nicely. How could this be happening? Why was this happening? There were no answers—none!

He put the car in gear and drove out of the parking lot. He didn't know where he was going, but he needed to move. He didn't know what he was doing, but he didn't think it mattered much. He drove aimlessly but with intensity—trying to flee the grip of the *other-world* as it tried to pull him in.

Twenty minutes later he found himself going over the Mystic River Bridge. He opened the car window and prepared to throw the phone out. But he stopped in mid-way through the act of tossing the phone into the river and out of his life forever. It occurred to him that even if he threw the cursed device in the river, the countdown would continue. He felt sure about that. It seemed unstoppable and inevitable. So, he continued over the bridge to a future that was completely uncertain. Unlike the bridge, his life was completely unmoored.

He drove for another ten minutes and then pulled the car over to the side of the road. He felt trapped. He felt betrayed by the app, by his phone, by life. He sat on the side of the road staring at the phone.

"This all started with an app—a stupid app. I wish there were a simple way to undo all of this."

He held the phone in his hands. As he did, Jamal's words came hauntingly to his mind. The *other-world* was reaching out. *Fuck*, he thought, *it wasn't just reaching out, it had its goddamned hands around his throat!*

Suddenly a glimmer of an idea came into his head, touching his mind as gently as a feather. He took in one breath and then another; letting the idea grow into something like a premonition. He touched the App Store icon and began to scroll through the list of apps. What he wanted was something to undo this terrible mess and so he searched for *Undo* in the App Store. He knew this was a fanciful act on his part, but his life had left logical and sane some time back.

The phone seemed to tingle in his hand, as if something unnatural had seeped into or out of it—he wasn't sure which. He continued to stare at it and he saw that his search revealed several apps with that specific name, but one in particular caught his eye. It had a bright red slash through the word *Undo*. Slowly he read the description:

Do you want to start over? Do you want to get rid of unwelcome apps? Then our app is just what you are looking for! It automatically seeks out and removes any unwanted apps from your life. With one click, our program will reset things back to square one. What have you got to lose, except a bunch of bad apps?

Jordan downloaded the app as he sat silently, hopefully, expectantly in his car. He opened the app and hit the *Undo* icon. He closed his eyes and prayed. Jordan's mind suddenly wrenched as the universe unfolded and refolded upon itself. His vision blurred, and he had a moment of disorientation and then …

"Shit, shit, shit, I can't believe I missed it," Jordan shouted into the phone. "How could I miss it? My own father's birthday! Who the fuck does that? On his 75th birthday no less."

Introduction to
The Permanence of Things

It should be the obligation of every writer to mine the darker side of humanity and see what lies beneath the surface. For under the attractive carpet of grass that is our reality, lies a dark and dank world filled with things that crawl and hunt or get hunted.

"Words have no power to impress the mind without the exquisite horror of their reality."
—Edgar Allan Poe

The Permanence of Things

He wakes and the need within him is strong. The pull to go down to the basement is omnipresent. It will not go away. Not today.

He gets dressed and goes downstairs to the kitchen. He thinks about having some coffee and a bowl of cereal, but the compulsion, the desire, the need to go downstairs overrides any of these mundane matters. The basement is his sanctuary. Downstairs holds his treasures; treasures he has gathered over a lifetime. These objects, are, in fact, a reflection of his lifetime. Each item holds a specific memory. Each memory a page of perfect prose in an unfinished novel.

The stairs to the basement creak as he descends. The light switch is at the bottom of the steps, so he descends in darkness. But to Shawn, the darkness provides comfort and security. He likes dank, shadowy places—they shut out the noise that sometimes creeps into his head. As he reaches the bottom, he turns on the light switch, and his treasures are revealed.

The walls of the basement are unfinished; layer upon layer of stone rise from the floor to the ceiling. The floor is a smooth expanse of concrete filled with long rectangular folding tables and bookshelves. Each table and shelf are crammed with a hodgepodge of different objects—a matchbook, a coaster, a bar of soap, a seat cushion, various items with no seeming connection or pattern, but Shawn knows better.

He knows what it looks like, and he knows that someone walking down into his basement would think he is some type of hoarder. But that just isn't true! Hoarders are untidy, but Shawn is meticulous. Hoarders collect all sorts of useless stuff like old mail, broken objects, and the like.

Shawn does not hoard; he collects. He collects something from every place he has ever been, whether that is a home of a friend, a restaurant, a doctor's office, or a movie theater. It doesn't matter to Shawn, for each item is a memory and as he likes to say, "*Memories are precious. They are all we have.*"

He remembers how his collection began so long ago. *It was sometime after his thirteenth birthday, and his parents decided to move from their farmhouse in Holly Springs to the city of Raleigh. The move was just twenty miles, but to Shawn it was like they had moved to another planet. Everything was different. In the country, Shawn could walk for miles without running into anyone. He didn't really like people all that much, so this suited him just fine. Now, there were people all around him all the time. They lived in a row house in the city and there were cars, people, and noise everywhere. Everywhere Shawn turned, something pounded his senses. It was too much for him. Not only did his parents move him away from his home, they did it without warning! He remembered waking up one day and his parents told him they were moving in a couple of days and so he needed to pack up his room and quick. That was all the warning he had. His father had said something about his job, but the rationale was lost on Shawn. They moved quickly, and it left him no time to adjust. He never forgave them for that, and he made sure that the pain was repaid in full.*

The move to Raleigh taught Shawn a lesson, and it is a lesson he has never forgotten. He now knows that he must hold onto things more closely, lest they be stripped away without warning. He understands that people cannot be trusted. People will betray you. But things will never betray you. They are permanent. So, he collects artifacts from his life, from every place he goes. It doesn't need to be a big thing, but it must be something that enables him to recall the place and events of that place.

Most of the time it's easy, just pick up the stray coaster from the restaurant— "easy peasy" as his mother was fond of saying. He just tucks whatever item he likes into his coat pocket and no one is the wiser.

Most of the time is, however, the operative phrase. Shawn remembers being picked up by the police one summer night when he was sixteen. *They had seen him wandering the streets at night and took him down to the station because he fit the description of someone who had recently robbed a series of neighborhood convenience stores. It wasn't Shawn, and he told the police as much. His father had eventually retrieved him from the police station, but Shawn had to sneak something out of the police station before they left. That had been nerve wracking. He remembered searching around the station with his eyes for something to take. The innate desire was powerful in normal situations, but this was no normal situation, and so the need was even stronger. His eyes eventually fell upon the detective's desk, and he spotted a notepad within easy reach. It had some writing on it; all the better, Shawn had thought at the time. It wasn't just an empty pad, but something that the detective has recently written on! It was irresistible! He absolutely had to have it.*

The detective asked his father to come over to the front of the station to sign some paperwork for his release, and that was when Shawn made his move. He stood, pretending to stretch his legs, and he leaned on the desk and slipped the notepad discreetly into his pocket. He was sweating like a pig as he did it, but no one seemed to notice. After all, he wasn't a suspect anymore.

The notepad from the detective's desk now sits on a folding table in the far corner of the basement. Shawn walks over and picks it up and the mere act of holding the notepad sends a shiver of pleasure down his spine. He has a piece of that night in his hands, and no one can ever take it away from him. It is his memory and his alone. He holds it lovingly in his hands, caressing it, stroking it. He begins to feel a stirring in his groin and he puts the notepad down. He does not want things to go too far right now. He puts the object down like a mother putting her child to bed at night and then walks around the room, looking over more of his treasures. His eyes hovering over one item and then another. There is so much to take in! So many memories he alone possesses.

Absently, he walks through his past, touching one object then another, each object evoking its own memory. Some memories are good, some painful; but that doesn't really matter to him. His need is to simply capture the memory regardless of its emotional debris.

For Shawn, experiencing an event in the present, in the here and now, is almost impossible. As an event in the present unfolds, his mind is far ahead, thinking of how to capture the event in his basement memory vault. Real-time experiences are surreal to him; they are ethereal and dream-like. Events only become real when they can be re-lived through a physical representation. Shawn's reality consists of looking at the past through the lens of his possessions.

His eyes fall on the far corner of the basement. A light bulb burned out some time ago, and he keeps meaning to replace it, but never seems to get around to it. He walks over to the corner of the room now, for he has not been in this section of the basement for some time. He takes his time looking over one item then another. There is a comb from the barber shop his father had taken him to when he was younger. Next to that is a small sign advertising a sale on Excedrin. He took that from the nearby pharmacy a few years ago. On the shelf below is a pamphlet from the Department of Motor Vehicles. At the corner of the shelf is a reference book from the library. He picks up the book and considers it for a moment, then as he is putting it back on the shelf he notices a small dish sitting there. It must have been hiding behind the book. In the dish is a set of keys. He puts the book down and picks up the keys.

How wonderful, he thinks. He has not seen these keys in years, hidden as they were behind the reference book, and it takes him just a second to recognize the keys dangling from the simple key chain. They are the keys to his childhood home, the home stolen out from under him by his parents. Parents he does not miss now that they were gone. He has some of his parents' possessions down here if he wants to remember them but most of the time he does not want to remember them. He moves to the center of the room to inspect the keys better; they glitter like metal jewels in his eyes. Shawn caresses the keys and once again considers his old home. A craving begins to germinate in his fertile mind.

He recalls how the desire to possess physical memories took hold of him only after the move to the city, so he has nothing from his first home. Leaving his former home so quickly did not allow Shawn to take any meaningful possessions with him. Now there was a hole in his memory. All he had taken from the old house were a few clothes and some video games. He remembers that his parents had sold the house "as-is," leaving all the furnishings for the new owners.

Looking at the keys in his hand, Shawn knows what he needs to do. He needs something from that house. *Just a small thing*, he thinks. *Perhaps the new residents kept his old night stand? He doesn't know for sure but it's possible*, he thinks. What he does know is that he will get inside that house, one way or another.

Shawn begins to plan. He tosses out the option of just driving by and asking the people who own the house if he can drop in and see his childhood home. The new residents may be open to that, but that will mean he will need to engage in a prolonged conversation with strangers and that is too uncomfortable for him. He avoids intimate contact with people as much as possible. His job as a video game programmer and tester allows him to work from home and avoid such situations. Besides, thinking the option over in his mind, even if they let him into look around, he will be under constant surveillance. Taking something out of the house will be nearly impossible under such circumstances.

He will need to get into the house when the new residents are not home, use his keys (hoping they still worked) and search the house in private. Shawn knows this is a risky plan, but the need, the overpowering drive to get inside cannot be denied. The question is, can he deny the urge long enough to put his plan into action?

He drives to the farmhouse at various times over the next several weeks. He buys a pair of binoculars from a nearby sporting goods store and uses them to watch the house from a safe distance. The house looks very much the same. It has a new coat of paint, but otherwise it looks like he remembers. He sees two cars at the house and he determines that a young married couple and their child live in the house. They both work at jobs that require them to drive to work. They both leave the house each morning in their cars, and the mother takes their daughter with her, presumably to school.

The weeks of planning are a strain on Shawn. He finds it harder and harder to think clearly. The desire to get into the house is like a buzzing insect inside his head. He sits in the basement, but unlike times past, the joy of his possessions eludes him. This new craving overrides everything else. He starts taking sleeping pills to help him calm down. They quiet the buzzing in his brain but leave him in a stupor. He sleeps poorly most nights as he tosses and turns in bed. When he does sleep, he dreams of insects entering his skull through his ears and eating their way to the center of his brain.

Shawn wakes up from another fitful night's sleep and decides that today has to be the day. He can wait no longer. The need has become intolerable. It is an itch that must be scratched—until it bleeds if necessary. He has done his homework, or so he believes. He's scouted the house and the comings and goings of the family that live inside *his* house. For in his mind, it is still his house.

The morning is cold and overcast and it has started to snow heavy wet flakes, they fall like soggy corn flakes from the sky. Snow in any form is a rarity in North Carolina, and Shawn takes this as a sign of good fortune.

He eats breakfast and gathers up his things like the binoculars and keys. He also gets out a pair of workman gloves and a small axe. He will use the gloves and axe to break into the house if the keys do not work. Shawn intends to enter via the backdoor where it will be less likely that he will be spotted. The backdoor leads into the kitchen and he can start his search there. He believes that he will have several hours until anyone comes back to the house.

He is about to gather up his stuff and head to the car when his phone rings. Shawn almost never receives a call on his cell. He takes it out of his pocket and looks at the number. He does not recognize it and decides not to answer it. He turns the phone on mute and puts it into his pocket. He then grabs the binoculars and keys and heads out to the car.

As he drives to the farmhouse the snow falls harder, and Shawn needs to use the windshield wipers to see properly. It takes him a full hour to reach his destination—twice as long as he had estimated. But, Shawn doesn't panic. He has plenty of time to accomplish his goal. He pulls off the road a short distance from the house and takes out his binoculars. Both cars are gone.

He parks and walks around to the back of the house. Memories flood his senses. He recalls playing ball on the back stoop; throwing the baseball at the steps so that it would bounce back to his waiting glove. He remembers his father cooking in the backyard on a cheap Weber grill, and his mother bringing fresh, cool glasses of lemonade out to them. The memories hover in his mind for a moment and then melt away like the snow on his winter coat. He shakes his head to clear his thoughts.

He reaches the backdoor and pulls out his keys, but they don't fit. They must have changed the locks. As he considers it now, the young couple who live here now could not possibly be the people who had purchased the home from his parents. That was almost twenty years ago! He curses himself for not thinking of that obvious fact, but how can he be expected to think clearly with the constant buzzing in his brain? He needs to get into the house. Once he does that, he is sure he will start to feel better.

He decides to go back to the car to retrieve the gloves and axe. He looks down to the floorboard of the car and anger swells inside him. The gloves and axe are nowhere to be seen. Somehow, he has forgotten them! That stupid phone call had distracted him. How could he be so stupid? Again, he tells himself not to panic. It will be OK. Just get inside the house and silence the buzzing in his head.

He retraces his steps to the backdoor. The door has several panes of glass above the lock. He pulls down his sleeve over his right hand and punches the glass hard. The glass breaks, folding in on itself. He pulls his hand back and despite the shirt sleeve, his hand comes away cut and bloody, but Shawn ignores the pain and blood and turns the lock. He walks into the kitchen and takes a deep breath. *Every home has a unique smell*, Shawn thinks, *and this place smells like home—his home.*

Shawn moves about the house inspecting one item and then another. While the house feels like home, the individual objects within its confines feel alien to him. It has been too many years since he had lived here, and all the home's furnishings are new and different. It disturbs him. It makes him angry that there are intruders in his house acting like the place is theirs.

Shawn climbs the stairs and heads for the bedrooms. The old stairs creak as he ascends, announcing his presence to the bedrooms upstairs. He doesn't expect the upstairs to feel any different, but he needs to see. There are three bedrooms, he remembers the layout quite well, and Shawn goes into each, looking, inspecting, picking up objects as he goes. He touches those he cannot pick up. Nothing! It all feels so empty to him. He is profoundly disappointed.

He needs something to take with him. The buzzing in his head is a constant reminder of that need. Then, from the corner of the smallest bedroom he thinks he hears a sound. He looks once again in the room and sees nothing that could have made a sound. He opens the closet door and finds nothing but a young girl's clothes. He looks under the bed, just in case, but again he finds nothing that could have created the sound. Instead, he finds what appears to be a large doll stuffed under the bed. He tries to pull it out, wanting a closer look. It is wedged tightly under the bed, and Shawn really struggles to get it out. It feels very heavy for a stuffed doll. He flops the doll on the bed and looks it over. It is a curious item, it has those eyes that seem to follow you wherever you go. *Great craftmanship*, Shawn thinks.

He stares back at the doll. He sits down next to the doll and caresses its hair. It feels fine and soft to his touch. *Truly wonderful workmanship,*

Shawn thinks. He decides right then and there that this is what he will take with him. For reasons that he cannot quite explain, this doll feels good to him. He knows it was never his doll. His mental faculties are fuzzy right now, but he knows this much. But, it is what he wants, and there is no one here to stop him.

Shawn stands and is about to lift the doll up off the bed when he has a sudden thought. Perhaps he doesn't need to leave right away. Why not stay awhile? The house is quiet, and no one is here. Why not? He decides to stay and see what it feels like to live here. It is, after all, his home.

Shawn descends the stairs to the kitchen. He turns on the radio and makes himself a cup of coffee. He thinks the radio will help drown out the constant buzzing in his brain. He finds a station playing soft rock and turns up the volume. He stares outside and sees that the snow is still falling. The backyard is accumulating a layer of snow. The music from the radio is interrupted by an announcement that local government offices and schools are closed today due to the uncharacteristic weather conditions. Shawn is only dimly aware of the announcement; he is contemplating his new home. He is lost in his thoughts. He knows that other people live here, but he just doesn't feel compelled to leave; at least not yet. Perhaps he will leave in time, but who knows for sure.

Absently he walks around the house, wandering from one room to another. He pauses in the living room and sees the doll by the living room sofa. Next to the sofa sits an old end table with a phone and a lamp. Did he bring the doll down with him when he went to the kitchen? He can't remember for sure. The doll seems out of place here. Again, he is keenly aware of the doll's eyes and how they seem to follow him as he moves. *How odd*, he thinks. He grabs the doll and carries it back upstairs to the bedroom. It's a struggle to get it upstairs.

He dumps the doll on the bed and looks around the room. For the first time he notices the decorations around the room. There is lots of pink with pictures of unicorns and one large stencil of a white cat with a red ribbon on it. The decorations make Shwn a bit uneasy, he will need to make changes here.

He stares down at the doll's life-like eyes. The doll is intoxicating, and he can't say why. He decides that maybe he will not bring the doll home right away. For some reason, he thinks that taking the doll home will be dangerous, and besides he needs to understand why he is so drawn to it. He needs to examine the doll in more detail. He thinks for a moment and realizes what he needs. He closes the bedroom door and locks it from the outside, returning once again to the kitchen. He's not sure why he locks the door, but for some reason he feels that it is a smart thing to do. He doesn't want that girl wandering off again. He laughs out loud at the odd thought. It's a doll, not a girl. Why would he think that and how would a doll wander off? People wander around, dolls stay put or at least they are supposed to.

Shawn rummages in the kitchen drawers searching for what he needs. After a few minutes, he finds a pair of scissors. *This will do nicely,* he thinks. *I will cut the doll open. I need to see what's inside of her.*

Shawn turns to head back upstairs. He is absorbed in his thoughts. He will get to the bottom of this. He must understand his fascination with the doll and have his new trophy. He knows that he came here looking for a new trophy for his basement, but the need to understand the doll has overridden this initial impulse. His head is full of buzzing bees, and he needs to let them out. He will open the doll up and then maybe, just maybe, he will use the scissors to open a hole for bees to escape his brain.

Shawn is so preoccupied with his own thoughts that he barely hears the sirens approaching the house. He wonders if there is a fire nearby. Are they fire engines or police sirens? He's not sure. In the end, he disregards the sirens. They are unimportant. They are not real. They are not part of his collective consciousness. He climbs the stairs one at time repeating, *"Memories are precious. They are all we have."*

Introduction to
Offense Taken

We are rapidly growing into a society that is offended by everything and everyone. Our moral outrage is disproportionate to the events of the day. What follows is speculative in nature, at least I really hope it is.

"Society exists only as a mental concept; in the real world, there are only individuals."
—Oscar Wilde

Offense Taken

He awoke to the alarm clock like a fire alarm going off in his head. He slammed his hand down in anger to shut it off, missed, and the clock fell to the floor. This only served to heighten his ire. He got out of bed and stretched, trying to loosen up. His arthritis was always worse in the morning, and today it was particularly annoying. The pain was most acute in his right hip. He knew why but knowing why didn't help ease the pain.

He decided to take a shower and try to calm down. Maybe a hot shower would also help the arthritis. As he stepped into the shower, the jets pelted his elderly frame. *Once this body had been a work of art,* he thought. Now, it was a shadow of its former self. The water felt good, but his mind kept drifting back to the events of yesterday and with it, his anger returned in full force. The indignity! The injustice! Anger seethed inside him boiling his blood. The anger, like some nasty horrible tenant, took up permanent residence in his consciousness. He paced back and forth in his living room, wearing a path on the carpet. His neck throbbed from the tension. He had to do something.

He sat down at the computer terminal he kept on the desk in the corner of the room. There was only one option available to him, and he was going to take it now. Justice would be served. He turned on the computer and launched the browser, finding the site he was looking for in just a few seconds. Of course, the Ministry of Offense and Injury was one of the top websites on the net.

He logged onto the site. However, he was not presented with a live Ministry Intake Agent to assist him as he opened the site to log a complaint. Instead, he was guided through a set of preliminary questions. At first this only piqued his anger further, but soon he understood that the preliminary questions were designed to ensure that his Intake Agent did not offend him in any manner. Thinking it over, he agreed that it was a wise precaution.

So, he carefully answered the questions, making sure to state his preference for personality type, physical appearance, and the general background that he preferred in his Intake Agent. The more he considered it, the more this made sense to him. He wondered why other businesses and organizations didn't adopt this strategy. God knows, he didn't want some happy-go-lucky, annoying, and physically unattractive person to appear on his terminal. The mere thought made him nauseous.

A few minutes later, a woman appeared on his screen. "Good morning Mr. Simpson. My name is Ms. Howell. How may I assist you today?"

Professional, courteous, but not overly chirpy—they nailed it, he thought. "I want to make a formal complaint."

"Certainly, Mr. Simpson. I just have a few questions, so we can process this to your complete satisfaction."

"OK," Simpson said. "Hopefully this will not take long," his general gruffness starting to assert itself.

"Not at all, Mr. Simpson. Let's just begin with a general summary of what happened. Can you tell me who injured or offended you? I know recounting such instances can be painful, so if you prefer to simply type your response into the terminal that is an acceptable method."

"No, I'll tell you directly, but to be honest just thinking about it drives my blood pressure up as high as Mount Everest."

She gave an empathetic nod and smile. "I totally understand. Please take your time and stop anytime it becomes too painful."

Simpson paused, took a deep breath to gather his strength, and began. "I was leaving a meeting over at 17th and Haven Street downtown. There's a production company there I am working with, and the meeting ended around 3 p.m. yesterday afternoon. The production company is putting together a documentary on late 20th-century societal impacts, and they wanted my guidance and input. Anyway, I left the meeting and got into the elevator. The production company is on the 25th floor. Anyway, here is where things went horribly wrong."

"Go on Mr. Simpson."

"As I was saying, I got into the elevator on the 25th floor and the doors closed. The elevator then stopped on the 23rd floor, and someone got in. The person, if you can believe it, walked into the elevator and did not even say hello! How rude. Right? Anyway, the doors closed and that is when I noticed it."

"Noticed what Mr. Simpson?" she asked courteously.

"The woman was sweating, profusely and she had a displeasing body odor! I had to ride with her and that god-awful smell for twenty-three floors. I just thank heaven above that no one else came on the elevator and had to suffer that assault like I did. Can you believe that? And to top it off, she acted as if she wasn't assaulting my senses. She never said a word and certainly uttered no apology."

"That's horrible, I agree," said Ms. Howell. She wrinkled her nose in sympathy. "Some people are just terrible citizens."

Simpson nodded emphatically. "I'll bet there are cameras in that elevator, and I'll bet they will collaborate the fact that she was sweating," he added. "I'll bet on it, just look!"

"Mr. Simpson, we will most certainly do that. We aim for a comprehensive investigation of every claim made to the Ministry. But before we complete the claims process I want to review your options. Would that be OK?"

"You do believe me, don't you? I have been terribly wronged; I have been mistreated and injured, and I demand that something be done!" His anger was piqued again, and he could feel his neck throbbing.

"Of course, Mr. Simpson. As I indicated, we simply aim to be as thorough as possible. I promise you that such a completely thoughtless and harmful act as the one you described will be taken very seriously by our team. Now, let me just review your options," she said looking down at her screen. Simpson could tell she was now reading from a script, but that was OK as long as he got some justice.

"First," she began, "you can simply apply for a general injury. In this case, the Ministry will evaluate your claim and make a payment directly to you that is commensurate with the offense you endured. Many people looking for a quick resolution choose this option."

Simpson, interrupted, "I see. But in such situations, the offending person doesn't learn a lesson. I want that horrible woman to understand the pain and insult she has caused me."

"I totally understand, Mr. Simpson. In that case, you can sue the individual for personal injury. After the incident is verified—and I am sure it will be—you can sue her for a violation of your personal space and well-being. We have handled millions of similar cases, and individuals who are so insensitive as to violate someone's personal safe space in such a manner are always in the wrong."

"In fact," she said, now looking up from her screen and the prepared script. "I just completed a case where, believe it or not, someone had the audacity to say out loud that people who are slightly less than the average height are, and I hate to repeat this because it is offensive, 'a bunch of Leprechauns.' Now, not only is that highly offensive to individuals who are vertically challenged, but it is also highly offensive to individuals with Irish ancestry. Anyway, I mention this only to demonstrate that we are very accustomed to handling these types of hostile remarks and actions."

Simpson nodded in total agreement, signaling to Ms. Howell to continue.

"If you decide on this course of action, The Ministry of Offense and Injury will of course pay all your legal fees and assist you in finding superior representation."

A small smile appeared on Simpson's face. This was more to his liking. He wanted to hear more, and finally he felt like he might just get some modicum of satisfaction. "Go on, Ms. Howell, is there anything else the Ministry would be willing to do for me?"

"Well, Mr. Simpson, there is a third alternative. If you so desire, you can file a formal criminal complaint. If you pursue that path, then the Ministry will take control of the case completely and investigate the offender. If it is her first offense in the last five years, then she will receive a fine. The second offense will result in a fine and six months' probation, but a third offense will result in five years imprisonment if the person is found guilty."

Simpson nearly jumped out of seat, which was no mean feat for an old man with arthritis and a bad hip. "Yes," he shouted, "that is exactly what I want. She needs to be punished. I want her to feel the pain she caused me. She must be stopped."

Ms. Howell, nodded respectfully. "We perfectly understand your desire for justice, Mr. Simpson. If you bear with me for just a moment, I will pull up the appropriate forms and we can get started. Simpson grinned a wicked little smile on his round face before turning his attention back to the screen.

"Now to begin, Mr. Simpson, I just need your full name for the record. After that, I have a few questions, and then the Ministry will take it from here and begin our prosecution so that justice may prevail and decent individuals like yourself can feel protected from such miscreants. So, let's start with your full name."

Simpson smiled a practiced smile, "My full name is Orenthal James Simpson, but you can just call me OJ. Everyone does."

Introduction to
Self Portrait

I leave the introduction to this story solely to Phillip K. Dick.

"It is sometimes an appropriate response to reality to go insane."
—Philip K. Dick, VALIS

Self Portrait

I try looking out the window of my small home but it's a futile diversion. I'm alone here in this small cottage except for Simon, my cat. Simon is a Korat, an unusual breed, but then again, he is an unusual cat. Smoke colored, his coat shimmers as he stalks around the house. Outside my window is a sea of white. Snow covers the front lawn all the way down North Street to the shore of Lake Champlain. It's not out of the ordinary for it to be snowing in Burlington in the middle of winter, but four feet of snow is extreme by most anyone's standards. The radio says it's a storm for the record books. Maybe it is, maybe it isn't. I only moved here five years ago from Syracuse, but it's the biggest one I've ever seen.

I try again to focus on the snow-covered surroundings. The snow spreads out like a fungus across the city, seemingly digesting the small houses, store fronts, and even the town hall as it falls from the grey sullen sky and grows upon the ground. The utter sameness of the vista is a poor distraction from the picture that hangs inside my bedroom wall. The painting on that wall calls to me; for it is me inside that frame. A call to myself from the bedroom wall, and I cannot dismiss the distant echoes from my past.

Moving here after Stephen was killed in the war seemed like a good idea, and I guess it was at the time. It was important to get away from that life. The life made back in New York when we were two, not one. That life is over now, but the memories, unlike flesh and blood, refuse to die. The war, by comparison, is a fading memory. I can barely remember V-E Day and the celebrations in Europe as the Nazis went down in flames. That was three years ago, I think. Funny how a world war that changed the course of history can more easily fade from memory than the pain in my simple little life.

Simon's insistent meows from downstairs tell me it's feeding time. As I leave the bedroom, I cannot resist one last look back at myself, one more glance at a reflection that isn't a reflection, but rather a ghost of who I must have once been.

I rummage in the kitchen and find some food for Simon. He eats greedily. For me, I get a bottle of bourbon out of the cupboard and sit down on one of the few chairs in the sparsely furnished main floor and drink.

I need to do something, but there is nothing to do and nowhere to go. My plan, such as it is, is to get stupid drunk, yet again, so that when I go up those stairs I can avoid my ghost, who will look down at me from my bedroom wall and remind me of someone who is long since dead.

The portrait had seemed like a wonderful present at the time. We had a few wedding pictures done before we got married and Stephen had taken one of those photographs to a local artist. He asked him to use the image to create a portrait of his "young bride," as he liked to call me, even though I was two years older than he was. Stephen told me that the artist had refused at first, saying that he required the subject to actually sit for him. How could he do justice to a portrait without a sitting subject? Stephen explained to the artist that he was about to leave for Europe. His unit would leave in a few weeks, and he wanted the portrait to be a surprise. The artist eventually demurred, but said that with a black and white photograph, he would have to do the portrait in subtle tones of gray and black—this was the best he could do. Stephen agreed.

Stephen brought the portrait home and with great fanfare we unwrapped it together. I was in awe. The picture was hauntingly beautiful. The artist had used powerfully defined strokes. On the canvas, numerous and subtle shades of gray and black swirled and danced together. At the right distance, they coalesced into an image that was me and yet not quite me. It was a different me, less defined but somehow more powerful. We admired the painting together. Stephen said that he now held two Ninas in his mind's eye, the real me and the painting. He told me that having two of me with him was bound to give him twice the luck in Europe.

A cruel joke!

Now Stephen is gone, but my oil-twin hangs on the bedroom wall reminding me of a life that could have been, should have been, and now, will never be. I should throw the damned thing out, but I just can't seem to bring myself to do it. I can't seem to even get close to the painting without growing cold and almost fainting dead away. Besides, the painting is me, but it's also my beloved Stephen. If I throw it out, it's like he dies all over again. I don't know. I drink. It seems to help. My eyelids grow heavy as the bourbon takes hold of me, and I drift backwards.

We found each other, of all places, at a fishing pier. I had come down to the pier to bring my brothers some lunch. We lived only a short distance from Onondaga Lake near Syracuse. My brothers loved to fish for trout on the lake. They would spend hours either on the pier or on a small pontoon boat we owned, fishing the day away. I strolled over to the pier and saw a man struggling to untangle his line. My brothers were a few yards away and throwing snide remarks in the man's general direction. I dropped off their lunch and said, "If you spent just a minute helping this poor man out, he might not look so foolish."

"Now where would the fun be in that?" responded my brother Robert, still smiling.

"Perhaps, if you attended to your own lines more, you might actually have a few more fish in that basket." I said pointing to their basket which was only half full.

Leaving my brothers to ponder that gibe, I walked over to the man. "If you want to untangle your line, set the rod and reel down on the ground. Then you can spot the problem and untangle it more easily."

"Is it that obvious that I don't know what I am doing?"

I glanced back in the direction of my brothers who were still laughing like school boys even though they were in their early 20's. He followed my gaze and then nodded, "I guess it is."

"I do so hate to see a man so out of his element."

"I am indeed that man. The name's Stephen Baxter, and I will take your advice. Although it might take all the fun out of the day for your friends back there."

"Those clowns are my brothers. Good enough fellows, but still a tad juvenile," I said in a voice that I hoped they would hear. "My name is Nina," I said extending my hand. We shook and I noticed his hands were calloused. "I am guessing that fishing is not your usual past-time. More of a farming fellow I surmise, and if that's the case, why are you down by the lake, rod and reel so ineptly on display?"

"You're an astute young woman," he said looking me over. His glance lingered. I understood it's meaning. "I work on the McAllister's farm about five miles northwest of here, if you know the place."

I nodded.

"Well the tractor is playing stubborn right about now and Mr. McAllister sent me down here to see if I could do some good while we wait for a part to be delivered to town. I hemmed and hawed a bit, telling him this wasn't my type of work, but he said that being as we were caught up on most of our farming duties, that I should make myself useful. If you know Mr. McAllister, then you know, he is not a man to argue with, especially if you want to stay employed."

I nodded again and smiled. He was instantly likeable, this man. "Well, not to offend, but you don't seem to be that useful down here. I believe a better use of your time might be to walk me back to town and tell me all about yourself Mr. Baxter."

"I do believe I will take your advice. Mr. McAllister will just have to understand, I guess."

"Oh, you won't go back empty-handed," I said and strode over to my brother's basket. I snatched a couple of trout out of their basket and dropped them into Stephen's. "There you go. You're all set." My brothers grumbled, but I shushed them both.

That was how we started. The two of us falling into each other, conforming to each other like a stream flowing into the ocean. I found Stephen so intriguing and acted (as was once my nature) accordingly. I was so sure of myself back then. I am so lost now.

My head hurts. My eyes are crusted shut, and I have to pee. I must have wandered upstairs at some point during the night and collapsed on the bed. I make a half-hearted attempt to rub the sleep out of my eyes, and I stumble to the bathroom to relieve myself. I meander back into the bedroom and peer out the window. It's dark outside. At least I was smart enough to bring the bottle of bourbon with me. It sits on my nightstand and calls my name. It's a call I don't want to ignore, cannot ignore; dare not ignore. I grab the bottle and take a long drink. I slide back into bed without staring up at myself. I hate myself.

The wind blows, and I stir. It is still dark outside. Is it the same night? How long have I been asleep? I feel something clawing in my head, but now everything seems a bit fuzzy. I look up, and I stare down at myself from the wall. I am so strange and unfamiliar. My hair is dark and wild, and it swirls against the canvas. I close my eyes. The painting seems to whisper to me. I open my eyes slowly. I see my hair growing and spreading like ivy along the wall. I shut my eyes and reach blindly for the bottle on my nightstand. I knock it over and some of the bourbon spills onto the floor. I scrabble for it, groping, I find it and pull it toward my mouth. I've lost some, but the contents still swirl inside the bottle, and I breathe a sigh of relief and take a long pull. I keep my eyes closed, but I can feel my oil-twin's hair slide across the wall. I can feel it from ten feet away! It is coming towards me. It slithers along the floor, seeking me out. In desperation, I slam my skull against the headboard and fade into emptiness.

The moonlight splashes across my face and I stir. How can it still be night? My head hurts. I can feel her staring down at me. She hates me. She hates what I have become. Is snow still falling from the sky? I can never leave this place. I can never leave this time. I can never leave this pain. I fall back to nothingness; it is a much better place.

I hear Simon meow, but from where? I guess he's hungry. Slowly, hesitantly, I open my eyes but my thoughts are diffused by despair and I am caught inside a dream—someone else's dream—I now believe. Simon is on the bed and then Simon is in the portrait. Simon is looking at me. Simon is looking at her. He is here and there, somehow at the same time. He stretches and his coat shimmers in the moonlight. I look for the bourbon, and I suck the dregs from the bottle as I try to get up. But, I fall back down on the bed. I am too weak to move, too weak to look away, too weak to feel. I lie there for a long time and alternate my gaze from the cat to the window and then to my alternate self.

I sag into the bed, it welcomes me softly. Slowly the bed pulls me down inside the mattress. Down, down, down, I slide. I can't breathe. I feel like I'm swimming straight up underwater desperately racing for air. I can't think. Simon purrs a mournful tune as I struggle. I pull myself up with no coherent plan. I flail and grasp for some purchase, somehow managing to pull myself up and out. It is pure instinct at this point. I fall towards the window and open it. The wind pours in, cold and unfriendly. The wind and snow encircle me in a frigid embrace. The snow drifts towards the picture and flows into it. Snow covers my portrait sister, my evil twin. She looks down with a mixture of scorn and pity. I look up with fear, and awe and nothing is real except the way that I feel.

I look up at the ceiling. I must have collapsed on the floor. I left the window open and snow now covers the floor. I will myself over to the window and slam it shut. It is still night. It's always night now. There seems to be little trace left of who I once was. I clamber down the stairs to find another bottle of liquor and to feed the cat. I grab the bottle and take a long drink. What I thirst for is not inside the bottle, but I really cannot resist its call.

Simon meows at me. What is he trying to tell me? Is he giving me a warning or damning me to hell? I yell, "I fed you already. What do you want from me?" He turns and walks away in disgust. I can reason just enough to know that something has happened. A line has been crossed. I am not sure when and where it happened, but it did indeed happen. I'm stranded alone on the ledge and every attempt I make to hold on seems to only push me nearer to the edge.

I wander upstairs if only to say goodbye to who I once was. There is only the devil to pay now, and I am ready to go. I sit on the edge of the bed, and with beseeching eyes I implore her for something, anything, nothing. Perhaps just a glimmer of daylight. She stares at me with eyes that do not see. Simon joins me on the bed. From the window, a glint of dawn gazes in from the horizon, and a glimmer of the dawn gently brushes against the portrait and is consumed in her deepening eyes. The light dances across Simon who shimmers and then disappears. I get up one last time and join my twin in the never-ending night.

Introduction to
Balancing the Equation

L ast year, my wife and I went to a casino that had just opened across the river in Maryland. We walked around and decided to play some slots just for fun. However, before you can play the slots or any other game at the casino you need to obtain a "Club Card." Well it turns out I had a little trouble getting my card because the casino apparently had another Brad Center in their records, who coincidently enough was born on the same day as your humble narrator. I thought that was quite a coincidence. Or was it?

"Reality is merely an illusion, albeit a very persistent one."
—Albert Einstein

Balancing the Equation

Darren gaped with utter disbelief at the woman who stood behind the golden teller window bars. She was about fifty, plump but not overly so, however, she wore a tight-fitting polyester outfit that did nothing to flatter her figure, such as it was.

"I don't understand," he said.

"Well, apparently we have another Darren Montgomery York in our computer database. Now that is not so unusual in and of itself, I mean a lot of people share the same name but what's odd is that this other Mr. York was born on the exact same day as you," the woman said as she handed Darren back his driver's license.

"So, there is another Darren Montgomery York out there somewhere who was born the exact same day as me? Not just the same day, June 2nd but the same year as well?"

"Yes, indeed. He lives in Seattle according to our records, so I guess you are not likely to run into him here in Maryland. Anyway, in order for me to issue you a Club Card, I need to make a few notations in our records to distinguish between the two of you. Just give me a minute."

Darren looked over at his wife who was growing impatient with the conversation. Darren could see it in her eyes; her always impatient eyes. Taylor wanted to gamble. Of course, she always wanted to gamble or drink, and the casino offered the best of both worlds as far as Taylor was concerned.

"We'll be all set in just a couple minutes, OK?" he said to Taylor over the din of the casino.

"Yeah, whatever, I'll wait for you over there by the dollar slots. Just hurry up already."

Darren knew coming here was a mistake, but it was impossible to keep Taylor away once the casino had opened last month. Up until then they had to drive all the way to West Virginia so that Taylor could get her gambling fix. That had been a three-hour ride. The Maryland casino was just twenty minutes from their home in Alexandria, Virginia. Darren had actually been very thankful that the nearest casino had been three hours away. It had provided a reasonable excuse to limit Taylor's gambling trips. Darren didn't hate gambling. In fact, he kind of enjoyed it now and then, but he feared Taylor was an addict in waiting, and with a casino now only twenty minutes away, her longing would be too easily satiated.

He stood by the teller window as the plump woman finished tapping the keys on her computer. She handed the Club Card to Darren.

"You're all set sweetie. Enjoy your evening and good luck."

Darren took the card and leaned towards the teller. "Seattle you say?"

She looked at him and gave him a knowing glance. "I know, I'd be curious too."

"Can you tell me anything more?"

"Sorry hon, I wish I could, but I can't say anything else. I probably shouldn't have said anything at all."

Darren frowned and went to join Taylor by the slot machines. Taylor was frowning as well, but this was a result of her impatience and had nothing to do with Darren's mysterious namesake. Darren handed Taylor the Club Card and her frown disappeared just like the money she was about to lose.

Darren abstractedly watched Taylor play the slots. She won $10 on the first spin but that was not a harbinger of things to come. She then proceeded to lose badly, and her frustration mounted proportionately to the losses she incurred. Darren's mind kept drifting back to the mysterious other Darren somewhere in Seattle. Who was he? What were the odds of someone with the same exact name and birth date? It bothered him, and he couldn't say why.

"Darren, Darren, hey you big dufus, stop staring at the ceiling!"

Daren shook his head and looked down at Taylor. "What?" he said.

"I'm losing here, let's move to a different machine. I need some good luck and this machine's run dry."

"Yeah, sure whatever. If you think the machines actually have luck stored inside them, then fine we'll move."

"Don't be such a jerk! Maybe if you would send some good vibes my way instead of day-dreaming about who knows what, then maybe our luck wouldn't be so shitty." Taylor said it with a sharp edge that cut right into Darren's psyche and he winced a little. He hated that tone and if the truth be told, he might even hate his wife. He didn't like the thought, but it was there inside his head regardless.

"Listen," he said, "why don't you go on and play. I'm going to walk around for a while. I'll catch up with you in say thirty minutes next to the casino entrance over there," he pointed in the general direction of the entrance.

"Make it an hour. I bet you my luck will change without your negative energy and I want enough time to win big."

"Fine," he said knowing that this was just Taylor's addiction talking. He'd probably have to go pull her from whatever slot she was in front of in an hour's time. He doubted she would actually meet him by the entrance, but he hoped he was wrong.

They parted, and Darren meandered around the casino. He kept thinking about his other-self out there somewhere. He felt like he just had to meet this Darren No. 2. He was curious. Well, truthfully, he was more than curious. He felt like it was kind of destiny they should meet.

He looked around the casino absently. So many desperate people searching for that one spin of the wheel or that one hand of cards that would change their lives forever. So many people trying to scratch an itch that was unreachable—trying to satisfy a boundless need. Taylor was one of them; out there in the crowded casino floor being sucked into the quicksand of this evil addiction.

He heard someone groan over to his left and glanced at an elderly man who had apparently just lost a big stake at the craps table. *The game*, he thought, *would never end for most of these poor fools*. Just as the thought entered his head, his thoughts turned back to Darren No. 2 as he now thought of him. Someone else out there with his identical name and birth date. He couldn't get the idea of finding Darren No. 2 out of his head. He started to wonder if he wasn't as bad as some of these gambling junkies? There was suddenly an inexplicable desire, an actual physical need to follow an uncertain path towards this other representation of himself. He felt compelled to do something. He started walking through the casino and suddenly found himself in front of the woman who had given him the Club Card less than an hour ago.

Darren walked up to her and gave her a flirtatious smile. "Hi, remember me?"

She looked at him for a moment, unable to place him. Then suddenly she smiled and gave him a little nod. "Sure, what can I do for ya?"

"Well, now that you mention it, I was wondering if you might be able to pull up my account on your computer? That is to say, anyone with my name and birthdate. I would really like to verify that you have my correct address in your system." The woman wasn't fooled, and Darren knew she wasn't fooled. They both knew what he was asking, and because they both knew, he pushed just a little harder.

"You have a beautiful smile. Did you know that? It's just this generous giving sort of smile," he said. "Do you mind if I ask your name?"

"It's right here on my name tag. It's Margaret," she said, pointing to it and now putting on a broad smile, just as Darren had hoped. Margaret knew he was only flirting to get the information he wanted, but almost no one ever flirted with her, given her appearance and the transactional nature of her work. It felt good, someone flirting with her. That feeling was something she longed for and she would prolong any encounter that allowed it to continue.

Slowly she said, "Well I suppose that it might be possible to look that up for you, but I can't share my computer screen with you—there might be confidential information on the screen," she said the final part with a slightest wink with her eye. She then gave her screen just a slight nudge as she turned her shoulder. It was just enough to give Darren a view of the screen. At the same moment, she exclaimed, "Oh my goodness, I dropped my keys!" She then bent down to retrieve the keys she had just purposely dropped.

Seeing this, Darren took his cue and took a closer look at the screen. He had just enough time to scan the display and make out the address of his namesake. It read 3102 Highland Drive, Seattle. And with that, Darren tipped a non-existent hat in Margaret's direction and headed off to where he and Taylor agreed to meet. Margaret smiled after him and wondered just what the implications would be from her actions. She would never know.

The next couple of days passed in a blur as Darren attempted to stay focused at work. He was a construction manager for the Ladd

Company based in Reston, Virginia. He had schedules to monitor, crew deployments to review, and purchase orders to execute and he couldn't concentrate on anything. His mind kept drifting back to Darren No. 2. He didn't know why, it was as if his mind had a mind of its own. After a week of futile attempts to stay on task he decided this mind-fuck wasn't going away and he'd better do something about it and quick.

He came home one evening and simply announced to Taylor that he was taking a few days off from work to visit an old high school friend who lived out in Seattle. Taylor didn't seem to care all that much, she simply wanted him to go food shopping before he left and to make sure the Club Card was sufficiently funded. He assured her he would take care of both items before he left. While he knew he was falling out of love with his wife and perhaps had already fallen, he would have liked her to care just a bit more about his sudden desire to get out of town. He might have liked her to ask even a single question about a friend in Seattle who he had never even mentioned before. But she didn't and that, in and of itself, said a lot about the state of their relationship.

He left two days later aboard a Delta flight out of Dulles International Airport and arrived in the evening on a cold rainy Seattle day. He rented a car at the Seattle airport and drove to a nearby hotel. He checked in and settled down for the night. Tomorrow he would check out Darren No. 2's house.

Early the next morning he drove to Darren No. 2's address. He parked a couple hundred feet down the block from the house and waited. An hour or so later, a man came out of the house and got into a small car and drove off, presumably to work, and Darren followed. The car was a bright blue Kia Soul and it wasn't hard to follow. The car parked in a lot operated by the University of Washington. Darren decided against approaching Darren No. 2 at the University. He obviously worked there in some capacity and Darren needed to see him in a more relaxed setting. So, he decided to approach him at home the next morning before he went to work.

The next morning Darren arrived extra early at Darren No. 2's house. He parked and walked up to the door. He then rang the doorbell and waited. He had no planned speech in his head and wasn't sure exactly what he was going to say. Strangely enough the compulsion to meet Darren No. 2 had been such a driving force that he really hadn't a clue what he was going to do or say once that door opened.

Then the door opened and standing in front of Darren was an identical twin. Darren No. 2, like Darren himself, was just over 6 feet tall, dark brown hair, slender build, with a round but pleasant face. He held a cup of coffee in his hand and stared at Darren. They both just stared at one another for a long moment.

Finally, Darren No. 2 said, "Well I guess you'd better come on in. I suspect we both have some questions for each other."

Darren entered and looked around Darren No. 2's home as they walked into the living room. The living room, dining room and study contained book cases that covered just about every inch of available wall space. The bookshelves held mostly text books and reference books on various scientific topics.

"Have a seat," said Darren No. 2.

"Thanks, said Darren.

Darren No. 2 noticed Darren looking with curiosity at the bookshelves.

"As you've no doubt deduced from the bookshelves and from tailing me to the University yesterday, I am a professor of physics at the University of Washington."

"You spotted me yesterday?" said Darren.

"Yes, it became pretty obvious soon after I left the house. I'm guessing you're not a private detective by trade," he said with a slight laugh.

"Well, uh, no, I'm a construction manager in Virginia. You and I have the same name and birthdate. Did you know that?"

"I surmised as much when I saw you at the door. How did you find me?"

Darren relayed the story of the casino and the matching names in the casino database. Darren No. 2 simply nodded as the tale unfolded.

When Darren completed his story, Darren No. 2 simply said, "Absolutely fascinating."

"So, who are you?" said Darren.

"I'm you or you're me. It really depends upon your point of view doesn't it?"

"I think I need a minute here. What the heck is going on? Do you have any idea? I mean, I really didn't know what I planned to say when I met you. I'm not even sure what compelled me to find you in the first place, but this particular situation was not even remotely in my head when I came to your house. So, since you seem less than surprised by all this, why don't you fill me in on what's going on here?"

"Darren, I am not one hundred percent sure I know exactly either, but I have a theory, if you care to hear it."

"I sure as shit want to hear it," was the only reply that came to Darren's mind.

"Good but let me ask you a couple of questions first. It will help confirm my theory and will give you the background you need to understand what's happened. OK?"

"Sure," said Darren. "Let's get started."

"Great, tell me where you went to school as a child. Tell me who your best friend was and who was the first girl you fell in love with."

Darren didn't see too much harm in giving out the information. Hell, it was probably out there somewhere on Facebook or some other social media site anyway.

"All right, Hudson Elementary, Rick Sutter, and Lisa Kauffmann. So?" answered Darren.

"Just hold on for a second, I have one or two more questions. Now tell me how your parents died."

"How do you know that my parents are dead?"

"Like I said, I'm you and you're me. My questions are premised on that assumption. So, again, how did your parents die?"

"Well, it's not a subject I like talking about, but my parents and I were in a car accident back when I was fifteen. My dad was driving, and we got rear-ended by a truck. Our car got pushed into oncoming traffic and well that's about all I remember. My parents both died in the crash."

"Exactly," responded Darren No. 2. "That is my story as well. What happened next?"

"I was in the hospital in a coma for two months, or so they tell me. Eventually, I got out and moved in with my Uncle Howard and Aunt Debbie. They were very kind. I lived with them until I was around twenty-three. They passed away a year or so after I moved out. Nice folks."

"And let me guess," interrupted Darren No. 2, "you don't have any other living relatives. Correct?"

"Yeah, that's right. OK, so what are you getting at? Are you really suggesting we are the same person?"

"Not exactly, I am suggesting we were the same person. My story is exactly the same as yours up until right after the accident. Unlike you, I didn't spend two months in a coma. I was out of the hospital in a week. I stayed with Uncle Howard and Aunt Debbie until I graduated high school. I got a scholarship to college and left for the west coast. I've never gone back east— never."

"Umm, I don't know how to say this to you, but I think you're nuts. Nothing personal there buddy, but really that is just bullshit."

"Really? Well, let's hear your explanation? Explain to me how we are both sitting here in my living room?"

It was a good question and Darren knew it. And the truth was, he didn't have a rational explanation. He didn't have anything that explained the fact that he was sitting in a house in Seattle with an identical twin he knew he didn't have.

"Can I see your driver's license?" was all he could say in the end.

Darren No. 2 reached into his wallet and pulled out his Seattle driver's license. It had their picture and their exact same date of birth. Darren got up and paced around Darren No. 2's living room. He eyed some of the book titles in the shelves: *Quantum Divergence*; *Inverse Dimensional Space*; and *Functional Asymmetry*. If the contents of these books were as obtuse as the titles, then Darren No. 2 just might know what the heck he was talking about. Darren found it hard to fathom that he could have ended up like his counterpart. He never took himself for the bookish type and certainly not a physics professor of all things!

"Darren, have you ever heard of something called the Mandela Effect?"

"No, ah. . . what, like Nelson Mandela?"

"Yes, like Nelson Mandela."

"What kind of effect are you talking about? I mean, Nelson Mandela was no scientist. He was a peace activist, a freedom fighter of sorts in South Africa. He ended up as their president if I recall correctly. I know that much."

"Well, let's examine those facts for a moment. There are a number of people out in the world who believe that there are different realities that can and do co-exist together. The crux of their argument stems from the fact that different people have different memories of public events—things we have all been exposed to during our lives. These historical events are remembered differently by large groups of people," he said and waited for some type of acknowledgement from Darren. Darren simply nodded.

Darren No. 2 then continued, "The Mandela Effect is the name for this phenomenon because it's one of the most famous cases. While you and I remember Nelson Mandela being released from prison and becoming the president of South Africa, many others believe that Nelson Mandela died in prison long before his release in 1990. Most of these people have no connection to one another but all of them remember or mis-remember Mandela's fate the same way. They are absolutely sure of it!" he raised his voice on that last point to make sure Darren understood the seriousness of statement.

"Now, the obvious temptation is to simply write these people off as individuals with faulty memories. The trouble is that there are whole groups who remember the same event differently than the rest of us. Their memory of these historical events differs significantly than our own but their memories are eerily consistent with one another"

He waited to see if Darren understood the point he was making and then added, "The Mandela Effect is the belief that there is actual evidence that people are experiencing events in different realities."

"That's simply a lot of jargon around the simple fact that people have shitty memories," replied Darren.

"Possibly, but let me ask you a couple of questions. First, have you ever eaten or remember eating Jiffy peanut butter?"

"Yeah, I think so. Why?"

"Because there has never been a peanut butter brand called Jiffy. It's Jif and it has always been Jif. At least in this reality. Do you recall the children's books about the Berenstein Bears?

"Yeah, are you going to tell me I made that up?"

"Nothing so jaw dropping but, in this time-stream it's actually the Berenstain Bears with the ending spelled with an AIN not EIN. Admittedly that's a subtle difference but the point is there are alternate memories out there representing alternate realities. There are literally hundreds of these misshapen memories out there. Some are really significant like the date of the shuttle Challenger accident or the actual location of Korea on the map. My point is not to argue the validity of the Mandela Effect, but rather to suggest that the concept of alternate realities is not so far-fetched as you might imagine." He waited for his words to sink in and then added, "Besides, do you have a better explanation for our current situation?"

"Let's say for the sake of argument that I agree with you. Great, we have a working hypothesis for this crazy predicament—fantastic! Now what?"

"A good question, and one solution is very simple; you go back to Virginia and continue on with your life. That's certainly a possibility."

"I guess I could do that. This whole thing has turned out to be more than I bargained for anyway."

Darren started to look in the direction of the front door when Darren No. 2's hand came up gesturing him to hold on just a moment.

"I said we could do that, but I didn't say that was what we should do. You see Darren, our existence together in the same universe does present some intriguing philosophical and real-world issues. The fact is one of us really doesn't belong in this universe. One of us slipped into this universe without permission. I am not sure how or why, but the facts are the facts. You are here, and I am here and one of us doesn't belong.

"What are you saying?" Darren asked, becoming a little concerned.

Darren No. 2 stood up from the sofa and walked over to the desk in the corner. It was covered with papers and his laptop. He opened a drawer and pulled out a gun. It wasn't a large gun, but it was menacing just the same.

Darren," he said raising the gun and aiming it at Darren, "I just think it might be safer if one of us was no longer in this universe. I don't want to harm you but there is an imbalance in the universe and I think correcting it makes the most sense. Don't you agree? With luck when I pull the trigger and kill you here, you will end up back in your universe."

"This is my universe!" Darren cried out. "You're the one who doesn't belong. There is no way I would turn out to be a book-head like you— one who apparently is also a psychopath!"

"Really, I hardly think name calling is warranted. Trust me, I take no pleasure in this act. It's really a matter of, how should I put it, correcting an unbalanced equation." He grinned, apparently pleased with the analogy.

"Look, you don't have to do this. I'll go back to Virginia. No harm no foul as they say. This is just crazy."

Darren No. 2, paused for a second, considered this plea and aimed the gun at Darren's chest. Darren was frozen. How could things have gotten so screwed up so fast? One minute they were talking philosophy and physics and the next moment, this man from another universe was about to blow a hole in his chest.

Fuck this, Darren thought. He stood and Darren No. 2's gun followed his movements. "I am not the imposter in this universe! You are, and I can prove it."

Darren No. 2's expression changed to one of genuine interest. "OK," he said. "Go ahead and prove it."

Darren opened his mouth to make his argument when there was an enormous thunderclap from the direction of the front door. Darren No. 2's head exploded right in front of Darren. Pieces of brain and blood went everywhere. Darren shuddered and then his gag reflex kicked in and he vomited copiously all over Darren No. 2's living room. It really didn't matter; the room would never look the same, in any event.

Darren lifted his head, spitting out the last of his breakfast and looked over at the front door. In the door frame stood another version of himself. Darren No. 3 he presumed.

Darren No. 3 walked into the house. "He was going to kill you. You know that don't you? I don't care what you were about to say to him. He was going to kill you."

"Probably, but how do you know that?"

"Because I have been watching him for over a month now and the man may have been a genius, but he was definitely not a good guy. You are the third Darren to visit him in the last month and he killed the other two dead away. I didn't realize what he was up to at first and then I had to get up the nerve to stop him. I saw you come to the door yesterday and I knew how this would end."

"Wait, there's me, you and two other guys named Darren that are now dead? There is or was five of us?"

"Yes, there are or were at least five of us and there may be more. I suggest you and I get the hell out of here and go figure this out."

Darren started toward the door and paused, "How do I know you aren't going to kill me?"

"You don't but the truth is, if I wanted to kill you, I would have done it already. The fact that you are still alive means I don't," he waited for that to sink in and then continued. "By the way, what were you going to say to our dead friend over there to convince him that you are the Darren that belongs in this universe?"

"I have no idea, I was simply stalling for time. I was hoping something would pop into my head. Fortunately, something popped into his head, namely the bullet from your gun."

Darren No. 3 grinned. He liked this Darren. "Listen, what I need is someone to help me understand this and figure out where we all belong. Are you in?"

Darren considered what he was saying. He knew that turning back was impossible now. He needed help and Darren No. 3 offered the only help available at the moment. They needed each other and for now that mutual need would have to do.

The universe seemed to be splitting apart and Darren seemed to be at the center of that fragmentation. Besides, now that the immediate danger had passed, he could feel the longing in him again just as he had felt it in the casino with Taylor that night. The same craving that pushed him to seek out Darren No. 2 in the first place had hold of him again. Some people got addicted to drugs, some to gambling, Darren was addicted to . . . well, himself, it seemed.

"Let's go," he said at last and off they went into the unknown.

Introduction to
DreamLife Inc.

I t has been said the road to hell is paved with good intentions. However, the following story offers a slightly different interpretation.

"Listen closely. . . the eternal hush of silence goes on and on throughout all this, and has been going on, and will go on and on. This is because the world is nothing but a dream and is just thought of and the everlasting eternity pays no attention to it."
—Jack Kerouac

---— ✣ —---

DreamLife Inc.

Richard Koniff was just sitting down at his desk when there was a knock at the door. Koniff nearly spilled his coffee as the knock startled him from his thoughts. It was just after five o'clock in the morning and normally the building was completely empty this time of day. As the Managing Director of DreamLife Inc., Richard liked to get to the office long before his staff to get a jump on the day's activities. DreamLife was now one of the most important companies in the world, and Richard recognized that strong and conscientious leadership would be the keys to its continued success.

There was a second knock at the door. This time, Richard stood behind his desk and called out to the unknown person or persons behind the large metallic door. "Come in," he said. "The door is unlocked."

The door opened slowly. Two men walked into Richard's office and sat themselves down in front of his desk. They didn't say a word. Richard looked over at them and slowly sat back down in his chair. They were dressed in everyday clothing, but their faces were anything but normal. Both men (for lack of a better term) looked almost alien. They were albino, with skin as white as copy paper, and they had no hair on their heads. That is not to say they were bald because being bald implied not having any hair on your scalp—no, these two guys didn't have any hair at all. No eyebrows, no eyelashes, certainly no beard or moustache because it looked as if they couldn't grow one even if they wanted to. But, there was something else—neither of them had any wrinkles or creases on their faces. Their skin was completely smooth and had a slight shine to it as if it were being lit from within. The only difference between the two was that one of them was at least a foot taller than the other.

Richard didn't know what to say, so he just sat down and stared. He had no idea who these people were or what they were doing in his office so early in the morning. He also had no idea how they had gotten into the office. When he said "come in" he had assumed that one of his team had gotten into the office super early to impress him and wanted a few minutes with the boss before everyone else got into the building. Well, he was dead wrong on that score and now he had two people in his office for God knows what purpose.

Richard was just about to say something, and it wasn't going to be polite, when one of them finally spoke. It was the taller one seated to Richard's right.

"Mr. Koniff, you must immediately close down DreamLife, Inc.," he said.

"What the hell are you talking about? Oh, and by the way, just who the hell are you, and what are you doing in my building at this hour of the morning?"

The two men just sat there. "I'll repeat," said the one to Richard's right, "You will need to shut down your entire operation at DreamLife Inc. effective immediately."

"Yeah, thanks for repeating that nonsensical demand. Now, you want to answer my questions and while you're at it, would you mind telling me how you two jokers got past my security system?"

"Mr. Koniff, those are all interesting questions to you, I am sure, but they are really beside the point." He continued, "You really must close down DreamLife, Inc. today."

"Do you have any idea what you are asking me? No, you probably don't," he said answering his own question. "I'll tell you this, I have no plans on closing this company for you or anyone else. But, I'll tell you what I will do, I'm going to call security right now and have you removed from my office and from this building at once."

"Go ahead and call whomever you wish. You will find that none of your phones or other communication devices will work," responded the one seated to Richard's right.

Richard tried his desk phone. It was dead. He stood up and pulled out his cell phone, no luck with that either. He reached over to his computer to send an email, and that failed as well. Richard collapsed back into his chair.

Just what the heck was going on here? This was now getting beyond weird and, if the truth be told, he was getting a bit scared. He looked again at the two individuals seated in front of him. The one to his right he mentally nicknamed Penn and the shorter one Teller after the magicians who were popular back when Richard was a young man. Since the shorter one never spoke, the nicknames seemed appropriate to Richard. Just what the hell they really wanted he wasn't sure, however, what he was sure of was that he wasn't going to accede to their ridiculous demand.

DreamLife was the result of fifteen years of hard work. He had poured everything he had into the company, and now when he and the company were on top of the world, he was being asked to simply pull the plug. Actually, as he began to think about it, he wasn't being asked, he was being ordered. *No damn way that was happening*, he thought.

"I just can't shut everything down. Thousands of people depend on DreamLife for their livelihood. Besides, do you understand what we do here? We have the most important jobs imaginable. DreamLife is life. That's not just our slogan, it is a fact. Without DreamLife and what we do here, millions of people's chance to live on would simply melt away."

"We are well aware of what you do here Mr. Koniff, and that is precisely why we came. That is exactly why you must close this business at once," responded the one Richard thought of as Penn.

Richard just stared at the two beings before him. The one to his left never spoke, and the other one never wavered in his demands. Who the fuck were these fellows? Were they from a rival company that thought it might be able to replicate DreamLife's process? He wasn't sure, and he didn't like the predicament he now found himself trapped in. He was used to feeling and being in control, and this situation seemed way beyond his control.

What they were asking was just about impossible. He had created DreamLife after years of research and development. Years he personally had spent in the lab. Richard had always had one goal and that was to prevent death. There were thousands of researchers spending time and energy on cures for cancer, heart disease, and other related illnesses, but Richard had decided early on in his career to take a different track.

His mother had died from pancreatic cancer when he was just a young man. Richard had been devastated. He could not free himself from that life altering moment. After her funeral, he had walked around in a fugue state for weeks. He recalled his sister telling him that right after their mother had died, she had been walking down the street and a dove flew right out of a tree and directly over her head. A dove of all things, outside their house in Sedona, Arizona. His sister was convinced it was a sign that their mother was on her way up to heaven. Richard was unconvinced. Even then as a biology major in college, his belief system centered around the scientific method, not religious mythology.

While he outwardly dismissed his sister's interpretation of the event, it set his mind in motion on an equally audacious idea, but one backed by science, not mysticism. Need life simply end as the body failed, he mused? He recalled how his mother's body seemed to shrivel before his eyes until she blended into the sheets on her bed. In the end, nothing had been left but those sheets and a body that had once contained his mother. But while the cancer had ravaged her body, he knew that her mind had stayed as quick as ever, right up until the end. He therefore committed himself to ensuring that life did not end simply because the body refused to cooperate.

After years of research, he began to glimpse a possible solution. The key was keeping the brain alive after the body had failed. He dismissed the early research into cryonics as a dead end. Freezing people with the hope of future revival was not fruitful in his mind, and even if some of the obstacles could be overcome, such as cell destruction using advanced nanotechnology, the process simply deferred the ultimate goal— the continuation of life. No, to Richard, the answer lay in keeping the brain alive.

Richard's line of inquiry led him to take risks with the brain itself. To pursue this particular avenue of research, Richard had to make a deal with the government. The government took care of the dirty business of finding volunteers for Richard's research. At least, Richard assumed all the people were volunteers. In truth, he never asked. He was truly single-minded in his thinking and had little time for such moral wanderings.

His research took years of painstaking trial and error. But eventually he and his team reached the stage where they had achieved some success. Richard found that the brain could be removed from the body before death and kept alive in an exactly balanced nutrient rich environment. But, keeping the brain alive did not necessarily mean true consciousness in the way we experience it during life. His next efforts focused on providing the brain with tiny electrical impulses at regular intervals. These impulses, Richard knew, were the key to normal brain activity, including conscious thought and memory. The brain's normal functions also included bodily functions such as regulating blood flow and body temperature, breathing, fighting off infection, and digesting food. However, with the brain removed, it no longer needed to concern itself with these more mundane activities.

Repeatedly, he and his team tried to achieve complete consciousness, and each time that ultimate goal eluded them. The team used extremely sensitive instruments to measure brain activity and each time the instruments demonstrated results just short of total consciousness.

One night, Richard awoke from an extremely vivid dream. In the dream, he and his mother were once again united. They talked and joked around. Suddenly, they were at a nearby lake close to Richard's current home. Intellectually, Richard knew his mother had never been to this lake, but it didn't matter, the dream provided the opportunity to share this new memory. Richard awoke with a renewed purpose.

The next day, Richard gathered his team and drove the work in a slightly new direction—toward bringing the brain into a dream-like state. By subtle manipulation, both chemical and electrical, the team eventually achieved such an outcome. In this state, the individual did not retain total consciousness or possess the ability to communicate but continued via a series of vivid dreams. While true rational thought was beyond his grasp, Richard's work enabled a person to continue in this dream state practically forever. Life after death now consisted of a continuous set of dreams, changing every time a new electrical pulse was supplied to the brain.

"Mr. Koniff?" said the individual Richard had nicknamed Penn. Richard turned his attention back to the two intruders in his office. His mind had wandered, but now he was focused back on the problem of the moment.

"Listen, all my adult life I've had just one goal—to extend life. I had to fight to get the government to approve DreamLife and since that day fifteen years ago, DreamLife has gone on to become the largest single corporation in the world. We are responsible for over fifty million souls! Do you understand that?"

"Mr. Koniff, of course we understand that. We understand that better than you might think." It was at this point that both individuals stood up and took off their jackets. Richard could see underneath their white shirts that their skin glowed. Their bodies seemed to pulse underneath their clothes.

Richard tried to make sense of what he was seeing. He was a scientist, and his mind was trained to dissect problems. What he was seeing was way beyond his comprehension, but it wasn't beyond his apprehension. He understood at once that these individuals were not human.

"What are you?" he sputtered.

"We are, simply put, what you humans generally refer to as angels. Although that description is a tad simplistic," said Penn. Teller, his companion, nodded in agreement.

"Angels?" asked Richard. He didn't know that he believed that, but he was still seeking understanding.

"Yes, and I can see the doubt in your eyes. To help, I'll send you a mental image of our true appearance. That should help."

Richard eyes closed despite himself. He saw flames flowing out from an intensely white-hot center. Richard knew his eyes were closed, but he reflexively shielded them with his forearm lest he go blind from the light. The light faded, and he opened his eyes.

"Angels," he said. This time it was not a question, but he followed that with the typical questions. "No wings? No halos?"

"No, that is all a human fabrication. We are pure energy. We have no real physical form, as you saw."

"OK, you're angels. What do you want with me?"

"You see Richard . . . may I call you Richard?" said the angel. Richard nodded, seeing no sense in standing on formalities at this point.

"You were quite correct when you said that you were responsible for over fifty million souls. But you see, that's our job, not yours. When you extract the brain of a person and keep it alive in those containers of yours, you end up fooling a person's soul in the process. The soul refuses to leave and proceed on."

"I don't believe in a soul," countered Richard.

"Your belief or non-belief is utterly beside the point. When a person dies, the proper channel for the soul is to return to the collective universal state. Our job is to guide those souls on that journey. When people see a bright light before they die, that's us they see. We are the bright light! We guide the souls in that process. Your procedure prevents the individual from moving on in any meaningful way. They stay tethered to this existence, but there is more for them to experience. Much more. The souls in your containers need to move on."

"There's some type of afterlife?"

"In a manner of speaking, but your process is preventing this. It has to stop." The angel's voice was firm, but not angry.

Richard Koniff couldn't believe what he was hearing, but at the same time there were two angels in his office and that kind of swept any doubt into the dust pan of rationality. Richard stared out the window of his office and looked skyward. He whispered one word in slow reverence.

"Mom."

He said it with hope. He said it with longing. He said it as the final note on the symphony that was his life. Then, Richard lowered his head, closed his eyes, and slowly nodded. He would close DreamLife immediately. What choice did he have?

Epilogue

I've always liked the following quote by George Orwell: "Reality exists in the human mind, and nowhere else." The only thing that would make that quote better (at least in my mind) is if I had said it. But alas, we must give credit to Mr. Orwell. Which kind of brings us full circle, doesn't it? If reality exists in the human mind, then it can be stretched by our imaginations. Reality then, is elastic in some sense. Now don't get me wrong, I am not suggesting that there isn't a physical world out there but let's have enough humility not to believe that we know all there is to know about our universe. As the old saying goes—the universe is not only stranger than we imagine, it is stranger than we can imagine. Keep that in mind as you go about your daily lives and remember there is always something around the next corner. The question is—will it be there to give you a hug or rip you to pieces? I guess it really depends on where your imagination takes you. Safe travels.

Lightning Source UK Ltd.
Milton Keynes UK
UKHW010725141218
333917UK00002B/31/P